A Cry for Vengeance

Ernesto Patino

ISBN: 978-1-62420-864-5

Cover Art: Designs by Ms G
Editor: Amanda Armstrong

Dedication

To Pamela

Chapter One

"So, what's this all about?" Sylvia Venegas strode into Helen Darby's house. "On the phone you sounded very mysterious." She followed her into the living room.

"Sorry if I alarmed you...but I need your advice." The obituary page of the newspaper with Karl Muller's name highlighted in yellow lay on the coffee table. "He was my patient...wasn't expected to live through the weekend." Helen stared at her. "Two days ago, as I adjusted his pillows, he reached for my arm. Then he said, 'I don't have much time. Please get some paper and write what I have to say.' I did as he asked and sat beside him. At first, I thought it might be something he wished to convey to a friend or a relative." She shook her head. "Far from it."

"Wh-what did he say?"

"See for yourself." Helen opened a folder, pulled out the handwritten note, and handed it to her.

My true name is Franz Dietrich. From 1942 through 1943, I participated in the extermination of thousands of Jews and undesirables at Treblinka concentration camp. Following Germany's defeat, I, along with other SS officers, fled to South America where we assumed new identities. Later, with the help of a pro-German group known as the Aryan Knights of the Fatherland, three of us emigrated to America.

For years I lived in the shadows, fearing that someone would recognize me. Every time I read about a former Nazi being exposed and arrested, I wondered if I would be next. Thankfully, it never happened.

I have many regrets, and yes, guilt, about what I did during the war. But I can't change the past. All I can do now is confess my sins to God and to whoever will read these words.

Karl Muller

"It's a deathbed confession," Sylvia said, her eyes still fixed on the paper. "Have you shown this to anyone else?"

"Just my supervisor. She reminded me that he was heavily medicated. She told me to forget about it. But I don't think I can. I mean…sure he was medicated, but I could tell that what he said was the truth."

Sylvia frowned. "Makes you wonder why he waited until the eleventh hour to unburden himself."

Helen shrugged. "The question now is, what am I supposed to do? When I pressed Mr. Muller about it—moments before he passed—he gave no clear instructions." She sighed. "In my three years of working with terminal patients, I've never dealt with anything like this."

"He put you in a predicament, that's for sure." Brief pause. "I have an idea. I know someone… an old friend who interned at the State Department several years ago. Don't know what he can do, but it's worth a try." Sylvia half-smiled. "Give me a day or so."

"I knew I could count on you," Helen said, relief in her voice.

~ * ~

Sylvia called Helen the next day. "I just spoke to my friend…his name is Bryan De Luca. He wants to meet you. Turns out he'd once worked with an international organization that documented crimes against humanity. He's got your number. Good luck."

"Thanks, I'll let you know how it went." Helen hung up just as the phone rang again. It was Bryan.

"I assume Sylvia told you what this is about," she said, a nervous edge to her voice.

"She said you were concerned about what your patient—an ex-Nazi—had revealed moments before he passed. A deathbed confession, she called it."

Helen sighed. "I thought I was doing a good thing…taking down his last words."

"I'd like to see it. Sylvia gave me your address. I can be there in

2

thirty to forty minutes."

"That would be great." Helen nodded. "Look for the house with the yellow trim."

Thirtyish, tall, with tousled brown hair, Bryan flashed a quick smile. He followed Helen into the living room. They sat across from each other.

"Would you care for some coffee?" she offered. "I made it just minutes ago."

"Thanks, but I had a cup earlier."

She paused, then picked up Mr. Muller's confession and handed it to him. "Like I told Sylvia, he didn't say what I should do with it."

Bryan studied it for a moment. "Do you mind if I keep this?"

"You'd be doing me a favor." She attempted a smile. "So, what next?"

"I have a friend in the State Department who might be able to help. I'll reach out to him. It shouldn't be too difficult to run a trace on Mr. Muller, or rather *Herr* Muller. By the way, did you show it to his family?"

"I never met them. According to a neighbor who ran errands for him, Mr. Muller and his family had not spoken in years. They live in Phoenix and were notified of his death by his attorney. He had left instructions that he be cremated."

"If you don't mind..." Bryan paused. "Let's keep all this to ourselves. Wouldn't want the press or even the police to get involved, at least not just yet."

"Okay, if you think it's best." She let out a slow, steady sigh. "I feel a lot better. The matter is out of my hands, and I have you to thank."

He smiled. "I should be thanking you. Sylvia's not aware, but I took a yearlong sabbatical from the university where I teach, to work on a book that I plan to write...about the Nazis who fled to South America and other places, including the United States. They're still out there, you know. Sadly, only a few have received the punishment they deserve."

"Will you include Mr. Muller in your book?"

"If I can verify his information. Of course, when I'm done, I'll have to alert the authorities in Europe or Israel. But that's down the road." He stood up.

She walked him to the door. "I really appreciate your coming here. I feel as though a weight has been lifted from my shoulders." She hesitated. "If it's not too much trouble...can you keep me advised?"

He nodded. "Sure. Though, it may be a while."

Helen waited a moment before calling Sylvia. "Bryan left about five minutes ago. Wasn't sure what to expect, but he turned out to be a nice guy...put me at ease the moment he walked in the house. You weren't aware, but he had an ulterior motive for agreeing to see me. He's doing research for a book he plans to write...about Nazis who fled to other countries after the war."

"I'm not surprised. He's part Jewish, you know. Not sure if he lost any family during the Holocaust."

"He didn't mention it. Though, we really didn't talk much. After he read Mr. Muller's confession, he said he'd look into it." She sighed. "I'm just glad I'm no longer involved. It's not my problem anymore. By the way, I want to thank you for reaching out to him. If you hadn't, I'd still be wringing my hands, wondering what to do."

"Well, you can tell me more over lunch...on you, of course." She laughed.

~ * ~

From his home, Bryan called his friend, Jeremy Levinson, in Washington D.C. They hadn't talked in a while, and for the first few minutes, caught up on each other's lives.

Finally, Bryan brought up the reason for his call. "I'm doing research on ex-Nazis who fled Germany after the war. Does the name Franz Dietrich mean anything to you? He lived in the U.S. under the alias, Karl Muller. Before he died just a few days ago, he dictated a statement in which he confessed to killing thousands of Jews at Treblinka concentration camp. That's all l know about him, so anything you can dig up would be helpful."

"Franz Dietrich," Jeremy repeated. "Sounds vaguely familiar...give me twenty-four hours. I'll check our data banks from 1945 to the present."

"Thanks. I owe you one."

Chapter Two

Bryan heard from Jeremy Levinson sooner than he expected. "I found something interesting…" he said, his voice tentative. "Are you ready for this? Muller worked for American Intelligence after the war, which explains why he entered the U.S. without being noticed. Unfortunately, there's not much more we can do, mostly because his records were *conveniently* lost."

"That's it?" Bryan leaned back in his chair and let out a sigh.

"I'm afraid so. In making inquiries, I learned that the subject of Nazi criminals is one that certain people would rather forget, and with good reason. It would be hard to justify a policy that allowed ex-Nazis to live in this country as free men."

"So, what does this mean? That we should look the other way and pretend that their crimes are forgiven?"

"Stinks, doesn't it? Wish I could've been more helpful, but under the circumstances…"

Disappointed, Bryan thanked him and hung up. He waited a moment, then dialed Helen. He filled her in on what his friend, Jeremy, had reported. "Did Mr. Muller reveal anything about himself?" he asked. "I mean…apart from his confession."

"To be honest, I learned very little about him. He kept his thoughts to himself. Don't forget, he was heavily medicated and slept much of the time. I was assigned to his case as a replacement, a week before he passed away at his home." She paused. "I just thought of something. His next-door neighbor…Cynthia Ruiz, checked on him, almost daily. I'm sure she'd be willing to help you. I have her number. If you want, I'll ask if we can drop by, so you can meet her."

"That'd be great. Tell her…tell her I'm a writer working on a project about Germans who settled in America after the war." A harmless pretext. "Let me know when she'd be available."

Helen called about a half hour later. She'd set up a meeting at noon. "Can you pick me up?"

"Sure. See you around eleven-thirty."

They showed up at Cynthia's a few minutes early. About forty, slender, with long, reddish-brown hair tied back in a ponytail, she led the way to the couch. "Helen told me about your project?" She gave a nervous smile. "I'll be glad to answer your questions."

"First of all, I want to thank you for agreeing to see me. I understand you knew Mr. Muller fairly well."

"We were neighbors for almost fifteen years but never became friends. He was somewhat of a recluse. What little I know about him is what he divulged during the past few weeks before he passed. He had no relatives nearby, and few friends, so I offered to help him as much as I could."

"Did his family know he was sick?"

"Not until I called them about a week before he died. I found their numbers in an address book that he kept by the phone in the kitchen. His ex-wife simply hung up on me. His son thanked me, and his daughter said not to call her again. It didn't surprise me. They hadn't spoken in years."

"Did he say why?"

She shook her head. "All I know is that he wanted nothing to do with them. He said it on more than one occasion but never gave a reason."

"What about visitors...friends, other neighbors?"

"I only recall a man and woman who dropped by, usually in the morning. They were about Mr. Muller's age. I don't know their names. After one of their visits, I noticed some religious material they'd left on the coffee table. Of course, there was Rosa, his maid, who cleaned his house every other week. She had worked for him for years. She knew he had no family, and so she came by more often when he began to get really sick. Once, when I dropped by to deliver his mail, I happened to overhear them talking about her son who needed some kind of medical procedure that she couldn't afford. 'Don't worry,' he said, 'I'll take care of it.' The next day, he confided in me that he planned to leave something for Rosa, but nothing for his wife and stepchildren. I kept a backup copy of his will, which I turned over to his attorney. Mr. Muller left specific instructions that he did not want any kind of service or memorial. He requested that his ashes be scattered in a rose garden in the middle of the Catholic Cemetery on the west side of town. I did as he instructed. It was the least I could do. Rosa was there to assist me. She was kind enough to say a short prayer, which I thought was nice."

Bryan stroked his chin. "You said you helped Mr. Muller quite a bit. What did you do, exactly?"

"Everything from picking up prescriptions for him, to taking him to the doctor. I also shopped for groceries and sometimes made him a sandwich or soup from a can. My husband thought he took advantage of me, which is probably true. But I did it because it was the right thing to do. In a way I felt sorry for him. He was old and alone, with no one around, and so I did what any good neighbor would do."

Bryan nodded. "One last thing…did he ever mention the names of other Germans, perhaps friends that lived in other parts of the country?"

"When I went through his address book to look for his family's phone numbers, I noticed two German names. He never mentioned them, but I copied everything down, thinking I should call them after he passed, which I did. The numbers had been disconnected."

"Do you still have the names?" Bryan said.

She nodded, then got up and crossed the room to retrieve them.

"I'd also like the names and addresses of his ex-wife and stepchildren."

She returned with a sheet of paper that contained what he asked for. "I included Rosa's information. She knew him a lot better than I did. She lives nearby, in an apartment complex on Grant."

Bryan glanced through the page: Josef Bauer, Kurt Hofmann, ex-wife and stepchildren: Carol Muller, David Muller, Elizabeth Muller, and Rosa Morales. "What happened to the address book?"

"It was destroyed. About a week before he passed, he asked if I could clean out his office of all documents, files and miscellaneous papers. I placed everything, including his address book, in boxes. The next day, a shredding company showed up and removed them."

"When you went through his papers and stuff…did you come

across anything unusual or out of the ordinary?"

Cynthia thought about it for a moment. "When I opened a shoebox full of cancelled checks and receipts, I spotted an unsealed letter, postmarked New York City, 1949. Out of curiosity, I picked it up and read it. I kind of wished I hadn't. It was a rather personal letter from a woman named Gladys. The way she expressed herself, I could tell that she loved Mr. Muller. She'd not heard from him in weeks and wanted to know if he still planned on visiting her during the Christmas holidays. She enclosed a photograph of the two of them, sitting on the stoop of a brownstone." Brief pause. "I don't know why, but it made me sad. The letter was shredded, along with the rest of his papers."

Back in the car. "So, what do you think?" Helen asked.

"The German names certainly got my attention."

"You think they're the ones who came with him from South America?"

"If we believe what Mr. Muller said in his confession, I'd say it's a good possibility."

She became quiet for a moment. "It's strange that he didn't leave anything to his family. His ex-wife, I can understand, but his stepchildren...it makes no sense."

"You're right, which is why I'd like to dig up some more information on him." He looked at her. "I'm curious about Rosa Morales. Do you mind if we drop by to see her?"

She smiled. "Not at all."

~ * ~

"Did Mr. Sullivan send you?" Rosa said, when she opened the door. About fifty, with a roundish, pleasant face and almond-shaped eyes that complemented her soft olive complexion. She wore a beige linen housecoat that came down to the top of her shoes.

"Mr. Sullivan?" Bryan said.

"Mr. Muller's attorney. Isn't that why you're here?"

He shook his head. "We spoke with Mr. Muller's neighbor, Cynthia Ruiz, and she gave us your name. I'm a writer doing research on

German nationals, like Mr. Muller, who arrived in America after WWII. I just need to ask you a couple of questions. May we come in?"

She hesitated, then allowed them into her apartment. They sat in the living room, which doubled as a sewing room. "I do alterations," she explained. "So, what is it you want to know?"

"Cynthia said that you worked for Mr. Muller for many years," Bryan said. "What can you tell us about him?"

"I cleaned his house, and we rarely spoke. He wasn't very friendly. Not until about a couple of years ago did I see a change in him. I showed up at his house as I did every other week. When he opened the door, he looked disheveled and apologized for his appearance. He disappeared into the bedroom. I did not see him until I knocked on his door two hours later. He came out, clean shaven, well-dressed and with a trace of a smile that I'd not seen before.

"He took pride in his appearance and insisted on telling me why he answered the door, looking the way he did. He'd watched a program on TV the night before, that showed scenes of Bavaria where he was born and raised. It made him think of his family. His two older sisters and a cousin were killed during a bombing raid in the middle of the night. He began to drink and didn't stop until he passed out on the couch.

"When the grandfather clock in the dining room rang out, we stared at it for a second." 'It's lunch time,' he said. 'After you leave, I'll heat up some leftover meatloaf.'

'I'd be happy to do it for you,' I offered.

"While we waited for the meatloaf to heat in the oven, I set the table. He thanked me and then, to my surprise…he asked if I would join him. I didn't want to be impolite, so I agreed to eat with him. From then on, we ate lunch together every two weeks. Sometimes, I'd show up with a casserole and other times he'd go to the Deli and bring something back. We weren't friends, exactly, but I could tell that he looked forward to sharing a meal with me." She sighed. "He was lonely like many men his age."

"Did he talk about his past, before coming to America?" Helen asked.

Rosa started to shake her head. "Only once did he mention that he'd been an officer in the German Army. He said it almost in passing, and he never brought it up again." She paused, then got up and retrieved an old cigar box that she kept in the bedroom. "Mr. Muller gave this to me a few days before he got really sick. He told me to keep it for him." She handed it to Bryan.

The unsealed box contained numerous black and white photographs of Mr. Muller before and during the war. Bryan spread them out on the coffee table. A smiling Muller in uniform, standing next to a German Panzer caught his eye. In a separate box, a little larger than a deck of cards, a well-preserved Iron Cross and an SS officer's skull ring.

Helen turned to Bryan. "You think they were his?"

"Maybe." Bryan shrugged. "Not that it matters." After a moment, he placed everything back.

Rosa stared at the box. "When I asked Mr. Sullivan what I should do with the ring and medal, he said they were mine to keep." She shook her head. "I'm not so sure. Maybe I'll call his family in Phoenix."

~ * ~

A pensive look filled Helen's face as they drove back to her house. "The way Rosa described her relationship with Mr. Muller, made me wonder. She said they weren't really friends, but I think they were, in a platonic sort of way. Would you agree?"

Bryan nodded. "I just hope Cynthia was right...that he left something for her."

"So, what next?"

He thought about it for a second. "I'd like to speak to his ex-wife. She may refuse to talk to me, but it's worth a try."

"I know that my part in this is over..." She hesitated. "Would it be too much trouble to keep me in the loop?"

"Not at all." He smiled, then changed the subject. "When Sylvia first called, she said you've been a hospice nurse for three years. It must be very rewarding, if that's the right word."

"It is, though I admit, it's not for everyone. If you want to know the truth, I decided to become a hospice caregiver after my husband died from pancreatic cancer. We had just celebrated our third anniversary. It's hard to explain, but working with the terminally ill helped me cope through my loss and emptiness that I felt."

An awkward silence. "I'm sorry."

Minutes later, Bryan dropped her off at her house, then hurried home. He couldn't wait to check out the information Cynthia had provided.

Chapter Three

Bryan dialed his friend Jeremy Levinson and got his secretary. He left a message and the names of two former Nazis, Josef Bauer and Kurt Hofmann.

Jeremy called three hours later. "You're not going to like what I have to say. There are no files on them. Apparently, they were destroyed years ago. All I could ascertain was that they worked for American Intelligence shortly after the war, just like Muller."

"By American Intelligence, do you mean...the CIA?"

"Not just the CIA, but also the Military. I'll see if I can dig up some more information. If I find anything, I'll let you know."

Another dead end, Bryan thought. When the phone rang, less than an hour later, he took his time answering it. He recognized Jeremy's voice.

"Not sure if this is important, but I remember working with an Immigration investigator who'd investigated a number of cases that involved former Nazis living in this country. His name is Sam O'Hara, a WWII veteran, who saw firsthand what the Nazis did at Dachau and other camps. Last I heard he had retired and moved to San Diego. There were rumors that he planned to go to the press to make a big stink about how the CIA and other agencies had protected the Nazis. Whether true or not, it made a lot of people uncomfortable, to say the least. By the way, his old boss gave me his contact information. Here's his phone number..."

"Hold on." Bryan reached for a pen. "Go ahead." He jotted down the man's number and address in San Diego.

"Thanks. I think I'll pay O'Hara a visit. Maybe he can shed some light on Muller or the other Germans."

"When you call, mention my name. It's been a while, but I'm sure he'll remember me."

Bryan nodded. "I will. Thanks, again." He hung up, waited a

couple of seconds, then dialed O'Hara's number. No answer. He tried again twenty minutes later. They talked briefly and agreed to meet the next day at O'Hara's home in San Diego, a short flight from Tucson.

~ * ~

Bryan arrived in San Diego around 10:00 a.m., rented a car, and drove to O'Hara's place, just off the I-5 freeway. The man lived in a condo overlooking a golf course.

They sat in the living room across from each other. "Do you golf?" said O'Hara, a fiftyish, balding man with a thin mustache and a wide, suntanned face.

Bryan shook his head. "Tennis is my game, though I haven't picked up a racket in months."

"I took up golf when I moved here. I'm not very good, and I do it mostly to break up the day." He shifted his body. "So, how can I help you?"

Bryan pulled out a copy of Muller's deathbed confession and a sheet of paper with the German names his neighbor, Cynthia, had provided. He handed them to him. "Muller dictated the words to a hospice nurse, moments before he died. The names came from an address book that he kept by the phone."

O'Hara scanned the items. "They're on the list," he said, matter-of-factly.

"The list?" Bryan furrowed his brow.

O'Hara stood up and ambled up to the kitchen table cluttered with files and miscellaneous papers. He returned with a legal-size document and sat back down. "Almost every Nazi living in the U.S., including Muller and the ones you mentioned, is on this list. Josef Bauer and Kurt Hofmann both worked at Mittelwerk, an underground facility in Germany where they built the deadly V-2 missiles launched against England. They were Nazi officers who supervised slave laborers needed to assemble the rockets. To maintain discipline, they routinely beat or hanged prisoners for the slightest infraction of the rules. Thousands died from exhaustion, malnutrition and disease." He wrote their addresses on a 3x5 card and handed it to Bryan.

"Thanks." He glanced at the card. "How were they able to enter the country?"

O'Hara released a long sigh. "The short answer is that they lied on their immigration applications. Let me explain. After the war, the CIA and other government agencies were desperate to gather information about Russia and other communist bloc countries, and so they hired ex-Nazis to be their spies against them. The fact that most of them had committed crimes throughout the war did not matter or was overlooked—*for the greater good,* as one CIA agent once told me. To many, the new threat was communism; therefore, the end justified the means." He shook his head. "For years I tried to build cases against them, but I was thwarted at every turn. The law is very clear. If a person lies on an entry application, he is subject to deportation or possible arrest. But in the case of the Nazis, the CIA managed to sanitize their backgrounds." His jaw muscles tightened. "It makes my blood boil every time I think about it."

"So, what you're saying is that our government gave these criminals a pass just because they signed on as spies against our enemies?"

"Exactly. A few even applied for and were granted American citizenship. The best example is Otto von Bolschwing. As an aide in the Jewish Affairs section of the Nazi Security Services, he wrote an official paper called *Zum Judenproblem,* The Jewish Problem, in which he outlined a plan to purge Germany of the Jews. Hitler was so impressed by the report that he assigned a senior officer named Adolf Eichmann to work with von Bolschwing."

"*The* Adolf Eichmann?" Bryan said, disbelieving.

O'Hara nodded. "When I heard that Eichmann had been captured in Argentina, I assumed von Bolschwing would be next. All I needed was some corroborative data from the CIA to build a case against him. Well, to my surprise, not only did the CIA refuse to cooperate with the investigation, but they managed to convince my superiors that I should back off...for reasons of *national security,* they claimed. National security my ass! They didn't want anyone to know they had made a deal with the devil, so to speak."

"So, what did you do?"

"I resigned in protest. It probably wasn't the wisest thing to do, but I was tired of fighting windmills and getting nowhere." He sighed. "The bastards won. They got what they wanted."

Bryan stared at him for a second. "Any chance that someone will pick up where you left off? I mean, if what you said is true…"

"Not likely. It would take the support of a prosecutor with really big balls to go up against the CIA and other intelligence agencies. Maybe in a few years, when the old guard is gone..." He gave a half-hearted shrug.

"About the names that I showed you…" Bryan leaned forward. "I had planned to interview them, but after listening to you, I'm not sure it would do any good."

A short pause, then a nod. "You may be right. Then again, what have you got to lose? If I could, I'd go with you just to see them squirm." He chuckled.

~ * ~

Afterwards, as he drove to the airport, Bryan thought about everything O'Hara had said. The existence of a list of former Nazis living in the U.S. intrigued him, and he wished O'Hara had showed it to him. No matter, the man had identified Josef Bauer and Kurt Hofmann as bona fide Nazi war criminals. To think that no one outside the intelligence community knew anything about them or their crimes disturbed him. All the more reason to confront them and record their responses.

Chapter Four

The next morning, Bryan called Helen and got no answer. He hung up and tried again. She answered on the fifth ring. Her voice sounded weak, as though she'd been crying.

"You all right?" He swiveled his chair away from his desk.

A long silence. "I just lost one of my patients. She was a young woman who died of ovarian cancer. I got to know her, and it was like losing a friend. When I first started working with terminal patients, I was advised not to get too close to them or their families. Good advice. But in the case of Rhonda—that's her name—it was hard not to. She was a warm, sensitive person who accepted her condition as God's will. She prayed often and I could tell that it helped ease her pain, as much as the drugs in her system. Anyway, that's why I'm kind of in a funk."

"I'm sorry," he said, softly. "I called to give you an update, but it can wait until—"

"No, it's okay. I need a distraction." She paused. "I have an idea. Why don't we meet someplace, and you can tell me about it?"

"There's a coffee shop near your house, on Tanque Verde, just east of Grant. I can be there in twenty minutes."

"I'll see you there," she said, and hung up.

~ * ~

"I'm glad you called," Helen said from across the table near the corner of the room. "I wasn't sure if you meant what you said, about keeping me posted." She smiled and took a sip of her cappuccino.

He smiled back, then became serious. "Let me tell you the latest." He filled her in on his meeting with ex-immigration investigator Sam O'Hara and his claim that scores of Nazis, including Josef Bauer and Kurt

Hofmann were being protected by American Intelligence. "The man held nothing back, admitting he had resigned in protest because of our government's hands-off policy with regard to Nazi criminals." He sighed and shook his head. "Bauer and Hofmann were responsible for the deaths of hundreds of prisoners at the factory where they built the rockets that rained on England. Unfortunately, they will never be prosecuted or deported."

"Did the international war crimes tribunal even know of their crimes?"

"Probably not. Regardless, there's not much anyone can do about it. That said, I intend to interview them…maybe catch them off guard. O'Hara gave me their addresses."

"Do you think it's wise?" she said, a hint of concern in her voice. "You might be accused of being a meddler or worse."

Bryan shot back. "I'm a private citizen, and I have every right to speak to whomever I please. If anyone has a problem with that…" He gave a small shrug. "But first I need to speak to Muller's ex-wife who lives in Phoenix. It's not every day that a Nazi criminal decides to unburden himself. I'd like to know more about him."

"What are you hoping to find?"

He thought about it for a second. "I'm not really sure. I just want to talk to her and see what she has to say. Tomorrow, I'll drive to Phoenix." He crossed his fingers and held them up. "Wish me luck."

She hesitated. "Not to change the subject…but I've decided to take a break from my work with terminal patients."

Bryan reached for his cup. "Does your decision have anything to do with your patient, Rhonda?"

"No…well, partly." She looked away for a second. "I have to admit that her death really got to me. I never thought I'd say this, but working with dying patients has taken its toll. It made me realize that it's time to do something else." She sipped her coffee. "Beginning tomorrow, I'll be on an indefinite leave of absence."

"What will you do?"

"Get away for a while." She smiled a little. "I booked a week's stay at a small villa overlooking the ocean in Puerto Vallarta…kind of a spur of the moment thing. That's where my husband and I spent our honeymoon. We had always talked about going back, but we never did. When I return, I'll request a reassignment to another department."

"Well, whatever you decide to do, I wish you luck."

Later, as they got up to leave, Helen said, "When I get back…do you mind if I call? I'm curious to know what you uncover."

He smiled. "Call me anytime. Have fun in Mexico."

~ * ~

"Hadn't heard from you in a while," Sylvia said, the second Helen answered the phone. "How are things going?"

"Great. Bryan identified the two Nazis that Mr. Muller referred to in his deathbed confession. It's all new to me, so I'm glad he's agreed to keep me in the loop."

"Sounds like you may be spending more time together," Sylvia said, with a chuckle. "In case you haven't noticed, he's a catch."

Helen hesitated. "I've not told this to anyone, but a year before Stephen got really sick, he said that if something were to happen to me, he would never remarry. Looking back, I'm not sure why he said it. I made light of it and assured him that I had no plans to die anytime soon. He laughed and we never talked about it again."

"I think I know where you're going with this, but that was *his* promise, not yours. Besides, you really don't know if he meant to keep it."

"But I *do*. We were soul mates in every sense of the word. I really don't need another man in my life. It's as simple as that."

"Well, it's your life…" She paused to lighten the mood. "What do you say if we meet for coffee or better yet, a margarita at Don Julio's, near my house."

"Make it a margarita. I'm leaving for Puerto Vallarta in the morning. I'll tell you all about it."

"I hoped you'd say that. Meet you there in half an hour."

Chapter Five

Phoenix

Carol Muller lived in a 50s style bungalow with a faded, metallic sign on the door that said NO SOLICTORS. Bryan had thought about calling, but changed his mind, fearing she wouldn't want to talk to him. When he rang the bell and got no answer, he knocked in rapid succession. Still no answer.

Halfway to his car, he heard the door opening and he stopped in his tracks.

"May I help you?" said a woman with a thin, tired-looking face. She wore a simple gray smock over a pale blue dress.

Bryan forced a smile. "My name is Bryan De Luca. Your ex-husband's neighbor suggested that I talk to you." A harmless lie, he thought.

"What about?" Her eyes narrowed. "Are you with the government?"

Bryan shook his head. "I'm doing research regarding German immigrants like your ex-husband, who settled in America after the war. I promise I'll be brief. I just want to ask a few questions."

"We were divorced a long time ago. I have no interest in talking to you or anyone else about him." She stepped back to close the partially opened door.

"Wait," he said, almost shouting. "The real reason I'm here is because of this." He produced a copy of Muller's confession and handed it to her.

She took a moment, then said through pursed lips, "The coward. He should have done this years ago." She removed her smock and allowed him into her home, which smelled of Pine-Sol as though she'd just finished mopping the floors.

They sat in the den. "Just so you know, I didn't learn about his Nazi past until after we married," she blurted before Bryan could ask any questions.

Bryan nodded. "Tell me about it."

She ran her fingers through her grayish black hair. "I guess I should start at the beginning. I was living in Chandler, just south of here, with my two kids, David and Elizabeth. Their father and I had divorced three years before. At the time, I worked the four to midnight shift at an all-night diner. Karl was a regular, and I waited on him every time he came in. He seemed like a nice guy…easy going…well mannered. So, when he asked me out, I said yes. He was much older than me, but I really didn't mind. We married ten months later. Not once did he talk about his past. He loved my children and eventually adopted them. It was important to him that they have his name."

"When did you learn he was a former Nazi?"

"I was getting to that. About eight years into our marriage, I happened to overhear my husband talking to someone on the phone. He sounded really agitated. When he hung up, I asked him about it. He ignored me and walked away, muttering something under his breath. I thought nothing of it, until the next day when a man called and asked if I knew that my husband was a war criminal. Before I could answer, he hung up. For a second I thought it might be the same person who had upset my husband."

"Did you tell him?"

She nodded. "I mentioned it as we sat down for dinner. He shrugged it off as a crank caller or someone who'd dialed the wrong number. I said nothing more about it. You have to understand that at the time, I knew very little about his life in Germany. Sure, I knew he'd fought in the war, but that's about it. He said it was a painful time in his life and preferred not to talk about it, which was okay with me. Anyway, I put the whole thing out of my mind, but not for long. Two days later, someone rang the bell. When I answered the door, there was nobody there. I looked down and spotted a white envelope on the welcome mat. I picked it up. Inside was a handwritten note that said my husband was a former SS officer responsible for the deaths of thousands of Jews at Treblinka concentration camp. They vowed to kill him and anyone who stood in their way."

"They?"

"The note mentioned a Jewish group—don't recall the name—that had been tracking my husband and other ex-Nazis."

"Did you show the note to your husband?"

"Of course, and I asked him point blank. Is it true that you participated in the murder of Jews at Treblinka? He became angry and defensive. He kept insisting that as a German Officer he had no choice but to follow orders, whether he agreed with them or not. When I suggested that we call the police, he said absolutely not. He had friends in the government who would *take care of it,* as he put it.

"What friends," I asked, but he refused to say. He assured me that in a few days, there would be no more calls or threatening notes from strangers, and I should go about my business. I didn't want to argue with him, so I let it go. He was right. There were no more calls or notes from anyone, and we never talked about it again."

"What about your children…did you ever tell them about his Nazi past?"

She sighed and looked away, simultaneously. "About three or four years later, I found out he was cheating on me. When I confronted him, he vowed he would never do it again. I forgave him, mostly for the sake of my children, especially my daughter Elizabeth, who adored her stepfather. But then when it happened again, well, that was the final straw. We got divorced six months later. Shortly after, he moved to Tucson. I had no further contact with him. I tried as best I could to explain to my children why I had no choice but to divorce their stepfather. They didn't want to listen. When they talked about wanting to visit him in Tucson, I blew up and blurted that he was a former Nazi criminal who had murdered thousands of Jews during the war. Call him and find out for yourself, I said."

"Did they call?"

She nodded. "After talking to him, my daughter refused to speak to me the rest of the day. My son was more forgiving, saying he needed time to process his father's admission about his Nazi past. They eventually accepted it and had no further contact with him. My only regret is that I didn't choose a better way to talk to them about it."

"If you hadn't divorced…,would you have told them?"

"I don't know." She paused and shook her head. "Probably not."

Bryan hesitated. "I suppose you know that he did not include your children in his will?"

Mrs. Muller swallowed hard. "It was his way of punishing me."

Bryan chatted with her for a few minutes longer, then left and headed back to Tucson. When he stopped at a gas station just south of Casa Grande, he called O'Hara in San Diego. He filled him in on his meeting with Mrs. Muller. Curious, he asked if O'Hara had heard of the Jewish group that Mrs. Muller had mentioned.

"JFJ, Jews for Justice," he said, without hesitation. "An underground group of hardline Jews that locates Nazi criminals throughout the world, including the United States. Unlike Simon Wiesenthal's organization that seeks to bring them to justice, their sole objective is to kill the ex-Nazis. They act as judge, jury and executioner." He sighed. "When I heard that the bullet-ridden body of a man linked to the JFJ had been found in a dumpster near Muller's house, I knew it was no coincidence."

Bryan frowned, then said, "Are they still active?"

"Hard to say, mostly because they're so secretive. People clam up when you ask about them. Anyway, that's what I know about the JFJ." Brief pause. "I probably shouldn't say this, but if I had a way of passing information to them…" He stopped in mid-thought. "Never mind. I keep forgetting I'm retired." He chuckled.

An uncomfortable silence. "Well, I won't take any more of your time. Thanks for answering my questions." He hung up and gave himself a moment. O'Hara's unfinished sentence was difficult to ignore.

Chapter Six

The caller spoke in a deep monotone. "My name is John Silverman, an attorney for the Southern Arizona Holocaust Survivor's Center which was named in a will by a donor, Karl Muller, about whom we know very little. I was told you might be able to help us."

"How did you get my name?" Bryan said, a cautious tone to his voice.

"Mr. Muller's next-door neighbor, Cynthia Ruiz, mentioned that you had questioned her about him. Perhaps, we should talk in person. I know it's late, but it shouldn't take more than a few minutes. If you'll give me your address, I can drop by."

Bryan hesitated, then gave him his address.

Mr. Silverman showed up thirty-five minutes later. They sat in the living room.

Fortyish, with a rising hairline and a well-trimmed mustache, the man cut to the point. "When I talked with Cynthia, she said you were a writer working on a project about German immigrants. Aside from what she told you, did you uncover other information about Mr. Muller?"

A brief silence, followed by a sigh. "Look, you may as well know the truth. Mr. Muller was a former Nazi responsible for the deaths of thousands of Jews at Treblinka." Bryan stood and retrieved a copy of Mr. Muller's confession. He handed it to him.

Mr. Silverman looked at it, then gave it back to him. "Who else knows about this?"

"Mr. Muller's nurse and his ex-wife. By the way, she confirmed that he was a Nazi criminal."

The man paused. "What do you plan to do?"

"You mean with the note?"

"Not just the note but with the information you've collected on Mr.

Muller."

Bryan didn't want to reveal too much, at least not until he knew he could trust him. "I haven't really decided." He shrugged. "I'm not sure if anyone would even be interested in reading a book about Mr. Muller and other ex-Nazis. These days, people seem to be more interested in what the Russians are up to."

"I think you'll agree, it would put the Center in an awkward position, having to explain why they accepted money from an ex-Nazi." He paused. "Can I count on you to keep this information out of any book or article that you plan to write?"

Bryan looked at him. "You're putting me on the spot, but under the circumstances, I guess I can leave it out."

Mr. Silverman smiled. He left as abruptly as he had arrived.

~ * ~

"Got a pen?" said the caller, the moment Bryan answered the phone. The clock on his desk said: 9:13 p.m.

Bryan recognized O'Hara's South Boston accent. "Go ahead."

O'Hara provided the names and addresses of three witnesses who had agreed to testify against Josef Bauer and Kurt Hofmann. "I thought you might want to talk to them."

"Thanks, thanks a lot. I don't know where the research will take me—maybe nowhere—but if I can succeed in exposing even one Nazi, well…it would have been worth it."

"Glad I was able to help. By the way, when you talk to the witnesses, you can say I referred you to them. It's been a while, but you'll find them eager to talk to anyone who will listen to their stories. Unfortunately, I wasn't allowed to meet with them after I left the agency. Good luck and call me if you run into any problems." He hung up.

Bryan took a moment to review the witness' names: Arthur Kaplan, Key Largo, Florida; Isaac Epstein, Charleston, South Carolina; Samuel Adler, San Antonio, Texas. It was early still, and he used the time to make flight reservations and jot down some preliminary questions. He'd interview Adler first, since he was closest.

Chapter Seven

Arriving in San Antonio, just before noon, Bryan took a cab to Mr. Adler's residence less than a mile from the airport. "Wait for me while I see if someone's home," he said to the driver.

He strode up to the door and rang the bell. "Just a minute," said a male voice trying to quiet a yapping dog. Soon, the barking stopped, and a bespectacled, balding man opened the door.

"Mr. Adler?" Bryan asked.

"If you're here about the ad I put in the paper, I changed my mind. The Chrysler is not for sale."

"That's not why I'm here." He stepped closer. "My name is Bryan De Luca. I'm a writer, working on a project about Nazi criminals who fled Germany after the war. Sam O'Hara, who worked for the Immigration Service, gave me your name. He said you might be able to help me."

Adler's face contorted into a scowl. "He made a mistake. I know nothing about Nazi criminals. If you'll excuse me, I have work to do."

"But I thought—" The man closed the door.

For a second, Bryan just stood there. O'Hara had seemed so positive that the man would agree to talk to him. It didn't make any sense.

The cab driver sounded his horn.

Back at the airport, Bryan considered his options: return to Tucson, empty handed, or fly to Charleston to speak to Isaac Epstein. He chose the latter and arrived in Charleston late in the evening.

In the morning, he rented a car and drove to Epstein's place, where a guard in a booth-controlled entry into the gated community. A sign near the entrance said: VISITORS TO THE RIGHT. Bryan slowed and pulled up to the window. "My name is Bryan De Luca. I'm here to visit Isaac Epstein."

The guard got Epstein on the phone, nodded twice, then turned to

Bryan. "He wants to talk to you. Park your car and come inside."

Bryan made a U-turn and parked on the side of the road. He stepped into the booth. "I've come a long way to meet you," he said into the receiver. "If I can have a moment of your time…"

"Are you a salesman?"

Bryan hesitated. "Look, I'll be honest with you. I'm a writer working on a book about ex-Nazis who came to America after the war. I got your name from Sam O'Hara. Can we sit down and talk?"

A brief silence. "I'd like to help you, but I can't. I'm sorry. That's all I can say for now. Please don't try to contact me again." He hung up.

Disappointed, Bryan got in his car and headed back to the airport. Once again, he weighed his options: fly to Miami to speak to Kaplan and risk another rejection, or return home to Tucson. By the time he reached the terminal, he'd made up his mind. He took the next flight to Miami.

The plane arrived a little after 7:00 p.m., too late to drive to Kaplan's home in Key Largo. He checked into the nearest hotel and settled in for the night.

Later, he called O'Hara and filled him in on his failed attempts to meet with Adler and Epstein.

"They got to them," O'Hara said.

"They?"

"The bastards who sabotaged my case. I don't know how or when, but they managed to send them a message: shut up or else. You can fill in the blanks. That's the way they operate. I'm sure Kaplan will be no different."

"Well, I'm still going to give it a try. If he talks to me or he doesn't…" He gave a half-shrug. "I've got nothing to lose."

"I like your spirit. Just be careful and watch your mirrors when you drive out to see him."

"Watch your mirrors?" Bryan repeated, after he'd hung up the phone. Did O'Hara seriously believe he might be under surveillance? If so, by whom and when did it start? In a way he wished O'Hara hadn't said anything. He shook his head and let out a sigh. Tomorrow couldn't come soon enough.

Chapter Eight

The drive to Key Largo took just over an hour. He'd checked his mirrors every few miles and again as he neared the island. Kaplan lived in a mobile home community that looked frozen in time—forties and fifties—with plastic pink flamingos and wooden pelicans on lawns or front porches. Evidence that a gusty squall had recently passed was everywhere: fallen palm fronds, broken tree limbs and scattered debris. Kaplan's home sat in a cul-de-sac.

From his car parked nearby, Bryan spotted a gray-bearded man raking leaves. Could it be him? Only one way to find out. He got out of his car and ambled up to the house.

"Good morning," Bryan said, smiling. "Must've been quite a storm."

"We're used to it, though lately we've had more than usual."

Bryan glanced around. "Are you Mr. Kaplan?"

The man's eyes narrowed, slightly. "How can I help you?"

"My name is Bryan De Luca. I'm a writer, looking into the activities of two former Nazis, Josef Bauer and Kurt Hofmann, who ran the Mittelwerk facility during the war."

The names seemed to strike a nerve. "Did Mr. O'Hara send you?"

"As a matter of fact, he did."

"Then you know what we're up against. They warned me not to talk to anyone, but I can't keep silent anymore. It is my duty, as a survivor, to speak on behalf of thousands of workers who suffered and died at Mittelwerk."

Across the street, a short, stocky man emerged from his home, lit a cigarette and stood on the porch. "We can't talk here. There's a coffee shop in a mall, about three quarters of a mile from here. Meet me there at six-thirty tonight and I'll tell you everything you want to know." He stepped to the side and went back to raking the leaves and debris.

Bryan nodded, then returned to his car.

~ * ~

Bryan waited at the coffee shop for almost an hour. Kaplan never appeared. Disappointed, he drove back to Kaplan's place. When he got there, he found police cars parked in front.

"What happened?" he said to a young officer who looked like he'd just graduated from the academy.

"I'm not allowed to say. I'll have to ask you to stand back or move along."

"Can I speak to a detective? I have information that may be important."

"Wait here." The officer went inside. A moment later, a dour-faced detective came out and approached Bryan, standing next to one of the cruisers.

"You have something to tell us?" he said, curtly.

"My name's Bryan De Luca. I was supposed to meet Mr. Kaplan about an hour ago, but he never showed up. What happened, if I may ask?"

"We got a call about a gunshot at Kaplan's residence. When officers arrived, they found Mr. Kaplan's body. He'd shot himself in the head."

"I…I don't know what to say. When I spoke to him earlier today, he seemed just fine."

The detective's brows furrowed. "About this meeting you were supposed to have…tell me about it."

"First of all, I should explain that I'm a writer doing research on ex-Nazis who were allowed to enter the country after the war. Under the protection of our government, I might add. When I learned that Kaplan was a slave worker at Mittelwerk where they built the V-2 rockets, I knew he'd have firsthand information about atrocities committed by a couple of Nazis who ran the facility. That's why I came here…to interview him about them." He paused. "This morning, when I approached Mr. Kaplan in front of his house, he admitted that he had been warned not to talk to anyone and suggested we meet later at a coffee shop nearby. When he didn't appear, I came back to find out what happened."

"You say he'd been warned…did he tell you about it?"

Bryan shook his head. "All I know is that he took a risk by agreeing to talk to me. For him to take his life makes no sense. Something happened between the time we met and the time he shot himself. I sure would like to know what it was."

"Well, he lived alone, with no family in town, so we can only speculate about his state of mind before he pulled the trigger. By the way, he didn't leave a suicide note, which is not that unusual."

Bryan handed him his business card. "Can you do me a favor?" Brief pause. "Can you call me if you uncover anything suspicious?"

"Suspicious?" The detective raised an eyebrow. "We find a guy with a gun near his body and a hole in his head, with no signs of foul play…it's an open and shut case. Of course, we'll wait for the coroner's report, but I can tell you with a ninety-nine percent certainty that he'll rule it a suicide."

~ * ~

Bryan couldn't get Mr. Kaplan out of his mind. Suicide or not, his death left too many questions unanswered. What started as a quest to uncover incriminating information about Josef Bauer and Kurt Hofmann, had ended tragically and abruptly. Sadly, it had all been for nothing. That's all he could think of as he raced to the airport to catch the last flight to Tucson.

Chapter Nine

Too much on his mind from the day before, Bryan got up earlier than usual. He called O'Hara just after 7:30 a.m. "I'm back in Tucson. You're not going to believe it, but Kaplan is dead, from a gunshot to the head. The cops think it's a suicide."

"You're right, I don't believe it. Tell me what happened."

Bryan repeated Kaplan's words from their meeting. "He gave no sign that anything was wrong…about anything. For him to take his life makes zero sense."

"They were on to you."

"I'm pretty sure no one followed me. I checked my mirrors liked you suggested."

"That means they were watching *him*, even before you got there." Brief pause. "Look, I don't mean to scare you, but this might be the time to back away from this before…" He stopped himself. "I think you should give it a rest. Do something else, maybe take a vacation or spend some more time with your family."

"I appreciate your concern, but I'm not giving up. If anything, Kaplan's death has made me more determined than ever to expose Bauer and Hofmann. I still want to talk to them."

O'Hara offered no argument. "Just be careful and call if you run into any trouble." He hung up, leaving Bryan to wonder why he had yielded so easily.

The doorbell rang. Bryan brushed his hair with his hand. It was Mrs. Jenkins, his next-door neighbor, bringing his mail. He thanked her, closed the door and returned to the den. He went through the pile of letters and solicitations from a half dozen charities. A plain white envelope, with no postmark or writing on it of any kind, caught his eye. He tore it open and pulled out a typewritten note.

It said: *You're meddling in things that do not concern you. Stop your investigation or face the consequences.*

His first instinct was to call O'Hara, though he knew what he'd say: heed the warning. He read the note again and put it away. For now, he'd do nothing, at least not right away.

The phone rang and he answered it on the second ring. "I'm glad I caught you," Mr. Silverman said. "Questions have been raised about Mr. Muller and his Nazi past. I think they're making a mistake, but it's their prerogative and as their attorney, I'm duty bound to comply with their wishes."

"I don't understand."

"Mr. Feinberg, the director of the Holocaust Survivor's Center, will explain it better than I. He would like to meet you. Would you mind if I set up an appointment?"

Bryan thought about it. "I guess it would be all right. Make it around eleven." He grabbed a pen and wrote down the man's address.

"Thank you," Mr. Silverman said, and hung up.

~ * ~

Bryan smiled when Helen called two hours later. "You back already?" he said, pleasantly surprised. "I didn't expect to hear from you for at least a couple of more days."

A long sigh. "It's hard to explain, but after three days, I was ready to come home. Too many memories of Stephen, almost everywhere I went. I got back yesterday. But enough about me, how did it go…your meeting with Mrs. Muller?"

"She opened up to me only after I showed her Muller's deathbed confession. I learned a lot about him and his adopted children who turned against him when they found out he was a Nazi criminal." Brief pause. "Why don't we meet some place, and I'll tell you all about it."

"How about Fort Lowell Park…it's near the post office where I have to pick up my mail?"

"Sure. See you there in half an hour."

When he arrived, Helen was already there. She waved to him from a table underneath a tree—just beyond the well-preserved ruins of historic Fort Lowell, for which the park was named.

"Come here often?" He sat across from her.

She nodded. "At least once a week. Sometimes I bring a book or a magazine. If I had thought of it, I would have suggested a picnic."

Bryan held back a smile. "Maybe next time."

For the first few minutes, Bryan talked about his meeting with Mrs. Muller, his subsequent attempts to interview three witnesses with direct knowledge of Josef Bauer and Kurt Hofmann and the death by suicide of one of the witnesses, Arthur Kaplan. When he was through, he let out a sigh. "Sam O'Hara, the ex-Immigration investigator, is convinced the man's death was the work of shadowy figures who will stop at nothing to protect the ex-Nazis."

"You think it's true?"

He shrugged. "Maybe. I mean...why would Kaplan kill himself hours before we were supposed to meet?"

"I don't know what to say," she shook her head, "except I hope you won't try to interview anyone else."

"O'Hara gave me similar advice." He hesitated. "I wasn't going to show this to you but..." He handed her the anonymous note. "It was among the mail that my neighbor had saved for me."

Her eyes widened. "You should call the police, don't you think?"

"And tell them what? It's a veiled threat. There's nothing they can do. Besides, I'd have to explain how Government operatives continue to protect former Nazis. It would go over their heads."

"I see what you mean...still, you can't ignore the threat implied by the message."

"I take it very seriously, but like I told O'Hara, I'm not backing down. I intend to finish what I started." He caught a worried look from her and softened his tone. "Don't worry, I won't push the envelope any more than I have to." He glanced at his watch. "Sorry, but I have to go. I have an appointment on the other side of town in fifteen minutes. I'm meeting with Mr. Feinberg, the director of the Holocaust Survivor's Center that was named in Muller's will. Want to come along? We can go in my car and I'll bring you back."

She smiled. "Sure." They stood and walked out of the park.

Chapter Ten

After an exchange of pleasantries, Bryan and Helen followed Mr. Feinberg into a windowless den that had part of a wall covered with plaques and citations. In the center, a framed black and white picture of Mr. Feinberg accepting an award from the mayor of Tucson. They sat around a coffee table cluttered with newspapers and magazines from all over the world.

Mr. Feinberg crossed his arms. "So, it was you who took down Mr. Muller's confession," he said to Helen, who seemed caught off guard by his pronouncement.

She nodded. "He didn't have long to live. It was the least I could do."

Turning to Bryan, the man uncrossed his arms and said in a heavily accented voice, "I called for this meeting so I could tell you, personally, that we changed our minds. After a heated discussion with fellow board members, we have decided not to accept the generous gift from Mr. Muller's estate. I won't bore you with the details but suffice it to say our decision is final and unanimous. As much as the Center needs the money, we believe it would be wrong and immoral for us to accept his donation."

"I don't understand. What does that have to do with me?"

"We would like for you to make our feelings known, whether it be in an article or in the book you plan to write. In other words, we are asking that you do the opposite of what Mr. Silverman asked you to do. We want to make it perfectly clear that the Center refused to accept money bequeathed to them by a former Nazi."

"I have no problem with that, though it won't be anytime soon."

"That's fine." A hint of a smile crossed the man's thin, worn-looking face. "Thank you."

Helen looked at Mr. Feinberg. "If it's not too personal to ask..."

she glanced at Bryan as though for approval, "are you are Holocaust survivor?"

Mr. Feinberg rolled up his left sleeve to reveal an identification number on his arm. "My wife and two daughters died at Auschwitz. I was the only one to survive. For years I would ask myself, why…why me? One of the things the Center does is to hold bimonthly meetings where survivors can vent and talk about their experiences. They come from different parts of Arizona and New Mexico. We usually meet at a survivor's home where people can feel more relaxed than at the Center. You're both welcome to attend one of our meetings." He hesitated. "I wasn't going to mention it, but for a long time we've talked about writing a book about our experiences, and with you being a writer, well..." He gave a small shrug. "There's a meeting at eight o'clock tomorrow night." He wrote down the address and handed it to him.

~ * ~

"Thanks for letting me come along," Helen said as they drove back to the park. "I hadn't planned on saying anything, but my curiosity got the best of me."

"I'm glad it did. To be honest, I knew nothing about him, and I had no idea why he wanted to see me."

She paused. "I'd never met a Holocaust survivor. I wish we could have talked longer. In my safe little world, I can only imagine the horrors that he endured, not to mention the pain in his heart that he carries daily."

Bryan nodded. "I've met two other survivors, a man and a woman. The man was so traumatized that he refused to talk about his experiences, even to his closest friends. The woman on the other hand, felt a need to tell her story to almost anyone who would listen. So, you see, each survivor is different." He slowed to make a turn. "About Mr. Feinberg's invitation…should we accept?"

"I have no other plans, so I vote yes."

Bryan smiled, then said, "Do you mind if I make a quick stop? It'll only take a few minutes. My grandmother lives in a nursing home, just up ahead. I promised that I'd drop by to wish her a happy birthday. She turned eighty-three, yesterday."

"Not at all. What's her name?"

"Gwendolyn and she's Jewish. I say this because she'll probably ask if you're Jewish. She's still hoping I'll marry a nice Jewish girl." He laughed. "I'm Catholic, by the way. And so was my father. He died five years ago."

"Have you ever been married?" she blurted.

The question caught him by surprise. "The short answer is no. But I was once engaged to a girl I met in grad school. She called it off a month before the wedding. She admitted she was still in love with her ex-boyfriend. He came back into her life and wanted to resume their relationship. She agreed. I'd gotten her on the rebound, which most people will tell you is a gamble, at best." He sighed. "It's better to have loved and lost than never to have loved at all. Isn't that what they say? Not sure what it really means, but it gave me comfort whenever I felt the urge to feel sorry for myself."

"I didn't mean to pry…I was just curious."

"That's okay. I'm way over her. Besides, my grandmother didn't like her." He laughed. He spotted the nursing home just ahead, put on his right blinker and turned into a long driveway that led to the entrance.

Her plump, pinkish face broke into a smile when they entered the room. "Happy birthday, Grandma," Bryan said. The woman sat on a rocker, with a white shawl draped over her shoulders. He gave her a hug. "I want you to meet Helen. She's helping me with a project for a book that I plan to write."

Helen reached to shake her hand. "Happy birthday."

The old woman scrutinized Helen for a second, then asked, "Are you Jewish?"

Helen smiled. "I come from a long line of Presbyterians."

"My husband, William, and I were of different faiths, but it didn't stop us from loving each other, even when our families said it would never work. Well, we proved everyone wrong and had many wonderful years together." She glanced lovingly at a picture of him sitting on her nightstand.

"We're just friends, Grandma."

The woman smiled and winked at Helen. "Well, friends can become more than friends, just like William and me when we first started dating."

Bryan shook his finger at her. "You never give up, do you?"

"You can't blame a person for trying. By the time I was your age, I already had two children, including your mother. Love and marriage wait for no one, as my grandmother used to say."

They stayed and chatted with her for a few minutes longer. Later, as they drove back to the park, Helen asked about his grandmother's family in Europe.

"Most died in the camps, though she did have a cousin who managed to escape from Dachau. She lost track of him after the war, but never gave up hope he would reach out to her. He never did. I'll give his name to Mr. Feinberg."

Minutes later, Bryan dropped Helen off at the park where she'd left her car. "I'll pick you up tomorrow at your house, around seven-thirty."

She smiled. "I'll be ready by seven."

~ * ~

On his way home, Bryan thought about his meeting with Mr. Feinberg and the reason he gave for refusing to accept Muller's donation. It occurred to him that at least one person would want to know all about it: Carol Muller, his ex-wife. He called her the moment he stepped in the house.

"Are you sitting down?" he asked. "There's been an unexpected turn of events with regard to your ex-husband's estate." He repeated what Mr. Feinberg had said. "Mr. Muller's attorney will want to talk to you, so expect a call from him later this week."

"Does this mean that my children will stand to inherit his money?"

"Probably, unless he listed some other beneficiary that no one is aware of. The attorney, I'm sure, will give you a better answer."

"I...don't know what to say. After your visit, I didn't expect to hear from you again, and now you're calling to give me the best news possible. Thank you. I'm sure my son and daughter will have lots of questions. Knowing them, they'll probably want to talk to you."

Bryan nodded. "They can call anytime."

Her voice started to break. "God bless you. Your call couldn't have come at a better time." Her words trailed off as she said goodbye and hung up.

~ * ~

When the phone rang, Bryan glanced at the clock on the nightstand: 11:12 p.m. He sat up and reached to answer it.

"My name is David Kaplan," said the caller. "Arthur Kaplan was my father. I got your name from a detective who said you were supposed to meet with my father the day he killed himself. Is that true? Did you know him?"

"I knew he was a potential witness against two former Nazis, Josef Bauer and Kurt Hofmann, which is the reason I went to see him. I'm doing research on ex-Nazis living in this country. Despite being warned not to say anything, your father had agreed to talk to me about them. That's why his suicide made no sense."

"I agree. I know my father, and he would never take his own life...for any reason. If he had a problem, he would always talk to me. In fact, he called recently to say that he was being watched by the people who warned him not to talk about his experiences. That's why he bought a gun for protection, which I thought was a bad idea. He hated guns."

"Well, I did my best to explain to the detective why I didn't believe your father had killed himself, but he didn't want to hear it. Unfortunately, when the coroner makes his report, the results will be final."

"I think you're right. I wish there was something I could do."

Bryan released a quiet sigh. "Sorry, I couldn't be of more help." He hung up and tried to go back to sleep, but he couldn't. Images of Arthur Kaplan forced him to stay up a while longer.

Chapter Eleven

Bryan and Helen were a few minutes late when they arrived at the sprawling, ranch style home near the Foothills. "Welcome, my name is Maria, please come in," said the petite, soft-spoken woman who answered the door. She ushered them to the living room where eight men, including Mr. Feinberg, and five women, sat around an oversized coffee table. Mr. Feinberg stood and introduced them as his guests. "Bryan is a writer," he added. They took a seat next to him.

"Please continue, Mrs. Feldman," he said.

The woman nodded. "As I was saying, I was five years old and my brother was only six months. My mother and father had not explained why they had brought us to the Catholic Church in the middle of the night. A priest was there, and also a pretty nun who looked like my Aunt Natalia. I was confused and a little afraid. When my parents left to run an errand, I thought they'd be right back. But they never returned. It was the last time I saw them. We stayed in the church for almost a week before we were taken to a house in the country. A man and his wife who said they were friends of my parents made us feel welcome. They had three children, a boy and two girls.

"As the days and weeks passed, I would ask about my parents, and always, I would receive the same answer. 'Don't worry. They'll be back soon.' After two years, I stopped asking about them. By then, the couple had begun to indoctrinate me into the Catholic faith. I knew I was Jewish, but I didn't mind, really." She shrugged. "I was only a child. Later, when the war ended, I was sent to live with a Catholic family in Switzerland. My little brother, Peter, was placed with a family in England. I never saw him again. Years later, I found out that our parents had died at Auschwitz.

"My early memories of being Jewish never left me, and so at the age of fifteen I decided to explore my Jewish roots. It was a bittersweet experience for me because it brought back a ton of suppressed memories of my father and mother." She paused to wipe away the tears that trickled down her face. "In many ways, I'm still that little girl that was dropped off at the church."

Her lips quivered. "I think I'll stop for now," she said, softly.

Mr. Feinberg nodded, then said, "I'm sure most of you are aware that one of the things we do at the Center is to help survivors, like Mrs. Feldman, in their search for lost relatives. We are actively searching records and doing everything we can to locate her brother, Peter. So far, we've hit one dead end after another, but we're not giving up." He gave Mrs. Feldman a reassuring nod, then said, "Before we continue, I'd like to read a brief letter that I received from David Adelman, a survivor of Auschwitz."

Dear Mr. Feinberg,

I am enclosing a faded photo of a young girl standing on the porch of a house—date and place unknown. It was found by a fellow prisoner, underneath a plank on the floor of our barracks. The girl will remain nameless unless someone who knew her can tell us something about her. As you know, there are thousands of Jews, including entire families, who went to their deaths without anyone knowing who they were or where they came from. Please show her picture to survivors who live in your area.

Yours truly,

David Adelman

Mr. Feinberg put the letter away and handed the photo to Maria. On the back, someone had written, *Our Precious Angel*. She looked at it, then passed it along. Everyone shook their heads.

"Sadly, Mr. Adelman, who had been ill for some time, died last week at his home in Scottsdale." Mr. Feinberg waited a moment, then said, "Would anyone else like to speak?"

A balding, middle-aged man cleared his throat. "I've never talked about my experiences to anyone, so you'll have to forgive me if I ramble or lose my train of thought. I'm not sure where to begin."

"Take your time," Mr. Feinberg said.

"I was sent to Dachau, where I kept to my faith and prayed daily, at least in the beginning. The one thing that sustained me was the hope that someone would come to our rescue. But as the weeks turned into months, I stopped praying. God wasn't listening, or so it seemed. Thousands were being sent to their deaths, and still no one came. If I sound bitter, it's because I am.

"Some will say that I was one of the lucky ones, simply because I survived. Well, the truth is, I survived because I did what I had to do." He clenched his teeth and took a deep breath. "I dragged corpses out of the gas chamber, checked inside their mouths, and if they had gold fillings, I would remove them. Then I carried them out and shoved them into a crematorium. Did it bother me? Of course, but only in the beginning. I shut down emotionally and perhaps spiritually. You can't do what I did, day after day, and remain sane." He started to hyperventilate and gave himself a moment. "Yes, I was a Sonderkommando, a word I despise because people seem to think I had a choice. None of us had a choice. Like I said, I did what I had to do."

"We're not here to judge," Mr. Feinberg said. He paused for a moment, then turned to Maria. "Would you like to share your story?"

She took a quick breath. "I was fifteen but looked older because of my well-developed bosom. When we arrived at the camp, the women and men were separated. I was terrified and avoided making eye contact with any of the guards. As we marched toward a barracks, a tall, gray-haired SS officer took me aside. I recognized him as the father of one of my friends and classmate, a girl named Frida. He escorted me into a private office and told me to undress. I stood naked, praying silently that I would not be violated or worse. 'Look at me,' he commanded as he unzipped his trousers and began to masturbate. When he finished, he told me to join the others. The next day he had someone bring me to his office. Again, he ordered me to disrobe. He stared at my face, which I had washed as best I could, and he said, 'You look familiar. What is your name?' Maria, I replied, without making eye contact. Then he said, 'Now I remember. You were a friend of my daughter, Frida.' He glanced at a picture of her that sat on his desk.

"For a moment, I thought he would tell me to get dressed and leave, but he didn't. He made me pleasure him with my hand. I felt dirty and ashamed. This became a routine in the days and weeks to come. Of course, he would always give me a piece of meat and some bread each time we were together, and it made me feel even more ashamed.

"But the worst was yet to come. One day he told me he was being reassigned. He assured me that I would continue to receive extra rations. What he didn't say was that his replacement, a much younger officer, knew all about our so-called arrangement. He raped me the first time we met. From then on, I knew what to expect. Months later, when he saw my expanding stomach, he went into a rage. 'Get rid of it,' he shouted. I burst into tears. But how? I replied. The next moments, he balled up his fist and struck me in the stomach. I fell to the floor, bleeding." She sniffled and reached for a tissue. "I'm sorry, it's hard for me to continue." More sniffling. "I, too, did what I had to do, to survive."

Mr. Feinberg gave her a moment, then said. "Mrs. Goldberg, would you like to share your story?"

Her dark eyes welled up with tears. "I'm not ready. It's too painful. Maybe next time."

Mrs. Rosenberg raised her hand. "I'd like to tell my story." She looked at Mr. Feinberg. "I had just turned twenty-one when the Germans invaded Poland. We lived in Lublin, a small village where our family had lived for generations. When I suggested to my parents that we should go to Warsaw, a much larger city where we could hide with friends or relatives, my father refused to discuss it. He insisted that we would be safe as long as we went about our business. Days later, I sneaked out of the house and took a train to Warsaw. The Germans controlled the city, and I was immediately arrested. All I could think of was that maybe Papa was right. I should have stayed in Lublin. A young German officer interrogated me for over an hour. Then, I was thrown into a holding cell filled with other Jews who'd been taken off the train. We had no privacy or a place to relieve ourselves. I was afraid and cried constantly until one of the guards threatened to shoot me if I didn't stop crying. After three or four days, we were taken to the train station where we were herded onto a freight car. At the same time, an engineer quietly walked up to us and whispered, 'They are transporting you to an extermination camp. You must try to escape.' His words sent a chill through my spine. I will forever be thankful to him for the last-minute warning.

"When they finally closed the doors, I looked around the car and noticed a metal grate covering a small window. I took off one of my shoes and struck the grate again and again, until it loosened. At that point, a big man with strong arms stepped up and forcibly removed it. Fortunately, I weighed just under a hundred pounds, with narrow hips and a flat chest that made me look like a boy. I managed to squeeze through the little window, causing my dress to rip off from my body. I jumped out and landed on a wet, grassy area. I lay there for a few seconds, badly bruised and hurting from head to toe. Thankfully, no broken bones. I got up, half-naked, and ran toward the forest. I kept running until I spotted a farmhouse, where two children played in the yard. I walked toward them. Before I could speak, they ran into the house. Moments later, their father came out and told me to leave or he would call the authorities. Can you at least give me some clothes? I asked. Before he could answer, his wife appeared and strode toward me, carrying a dress. 'Take it and leave,' she said. I grabbed it and ran back the way I had come. I continued to walk through the forest, not knowing where I was headed. When night fell, I stopped to rest. I was beyond exhausted and slept through the night."

She paused, then continued. "In the morning, I knew I had to keep going. I walked for hours until I heard bells ringing in the distance. I picked up my pace and stopped when I saw an elderly nun cutting across a field near a convent. I rushed toward her. She turned and looked at me. 'We must hurry,' she said. I followed her to a side entrance which led to a courtyard and to a small room that would be my safe haven for the rest of the war." A brief silence, then a sigh. "I learned later that my parents, grandparents and younger sister had died at the Belzec Camp. Had I stayed in Lublin, I would not be alive today." She sniffled and fought to hold back her tears.

Mr. Feinberg turned to the man next to her. "What about you, Mr. Bormann, would you like to tell us your story?"

The man nodded. "I was eleven years old when the Nazis came to our house to arrest me and my mother, who was Jewish. Fortunately, I was not home at the time. My father who was Christian, told them that I had gone to play in the park. Even though I had a German surname and looked like my father, I was considered a Jew. They said he should bring me to the police headquarters as soon as I returned. The moment I walked through the door, my father told me about my mother and ordered me out of the house. 'Go to your Uncle Max and stay there until I find a better place for you,' he said, handing me a bag with some clothes and a few essentials.

"I stayed with Uncle Max for six weeks. By that time, my father had found another hiding place, a small farm owned by one of his friends. The man said I had to sleep in the barn, which really wasn't that bad. I rarely went out for fear of being seen by visitors and the police which made routine checks for runaway Jews. The man's wife was nice, but I could tell she was afraid. Not that I blame her. It was against the law to hide or give assistance to a Jew. I stayed at this place for almost three years. My father visited me at least once a month. All he knew about my mother was that she had been put on a train with other Jews and sent to a labor camp in Poland.

"I saw my father for the last time when he came to tell me that he had been conscripted. Despite the fact he had limited use of his left hand due to an accident where he worked, he was told to report to a military unit in Berlin. The Russians were approaching, and they needed every man regardless of age or disability to defend the city. Days later, I learned that the Russians had reached Berlin. They showed no mercy to the defenders, most of whom were old men and young boys. Later, I learned that my father was killed while trying to surrender." He paused to rub his eyes with his thumb and forefinger. "After the war, I searched for my mother. It took a while, but I eventually found her name on a list of prisoners who died at Dachau." He sighed. "I have nothing more to say except that I regret I never got to hold my mother one last time."

"Mr. Eisenbach, would you like to tell your story?" Mr. Feinberg said, after a pause.

"Yes," he said, barely audible. "My wife, Greta and I were high school sweethearts. When we married, I was nineteen…she was eighteen. At the time, there were rumblings about a possible German invasion into parts of Poland, but we paid no attention. We were in love and that's all that mattered. Within less than a month, everything changed. German soldiers were literally at our door. Every Jew in the village was arrested and taken to a holding area near the train station. Within twenty-four hours we were herded into cattle cars, bound for a detention camp where we would be allowed to work and remain for the duration of the war. That is what we were told. The camp turned out to be Auschwitz.

"When we arrived, we were separated and sent to different sections of the camp. I never saw my lovely Greta again. Through the prisoner network, I heard that Greta's health had deteriorated to the point that she could barely walk. Bouts of dysentery had taken its toll on her and other prisoners. By then, we'd heard rumors that the Germans were losing the war. Every day we expected to hear Allied planes releasing their bombs over the camps. It would have been worthwhile to die, knowing that our German captors would die with us. The days turned into weeks and still the Allied forces did not come. We had given up hope of being rescued. Not until we saw Russian soldiers approaching the camp, did we know that our nightmare was over. Weeks after recovering in a medical facility, I learned that Greta had been transferred to another camp just prior to our liberation.

"I didn't know whether Greta was dead or alive, and so I searched through dozens of records from other camps, but found nothing, which gave me hope she might still be alive. Then, one day, I happened to meet a woman who had been on an open rail car with Greta. She informed me that Greta had jumped from the fast-moving car and had probably died as a result. It was then that I decided to go to America to start a new life. I eventually met and married a wonderful woman. We have two beautiful children, a boy and a girl. The years passed, but I never forgot the girl who had captured my heart so many years ago. Then, one day, I received a call from a friend in Israel. 'Greta is alive,' he said. By some miracle she managed to survive one hardship after another. She thought I had died at Auschwitz. My friend gave me her phone number. It took a moment to process the information. Did she remarry? I asked, almost afraid to hear the answer. She had not."

Mr. Eisenbach closed his eyes and took a moment. "I waited a couple of days before calling. When I heard her voice, I burst into tears. We talked for almost two hours. She understood my dilemma with regard to my American wife and children and agreed to sign the necessary papers to end our marriage. It was difficult to say goodbye because there was so much left unsaid, so many questions left unanswered. Greta was the love of my life, and there was nothing I could do to make up for the years she spent believing I had died." His voice dropped to almost a whisper. "A week after the call, she took her own life."

The phone rang. "Please excuse me." Maria got up and disappeared into one of the bedrooms.

"While we wait for Maria…there's coffee, tea and soft drinks." Mr. Feinberg stood and led the way to the dining room table. Bryan and Helen remained seated.

"I have to say, that of all the stories, Mr. Eisenbach's really got to me." Bryan let out a sigh. "Sad, really sad."

"Poor man. His wife's death will haunt him for the rest of his life." She sniffled and brushed away a tear that formed in the corner of her eye.

Bryan gave her a second. "Let's join the others." They got up and ambled up to the table.

When Maria returned, everyone took their seats. After a moment, Mr. Feinberg glanced around. "Mrs. Goldwyn, would you like to share your story?"

The woman nodded. "In 1943, my sister and I were arrested and sent to Auschwitz. Because we played the violin, we were assigned to the women's orchestra which played for the workers, patients in the infirmary and for the SS on Sundays. We were used as a propaganda tool for official visitors and photographers. While other women toiled in factories, under unbearable conditions, we practiced for hours—that was our one and only job. We played every day, rain or shine. Our reward was that we would get to live another day.

"On a Sunday afternoon, the orchestra played for the infamous Dr. Joseph Mengele and his friends. We were told that he had requested one of his favorites, Beethoven's Violin Sonata No. 9. My sister, who seemed unusually nervous, was asked to play it. Her hands trembled as she picked up the violin and produced the first notes that sounded slightly off key. 'Stop,' Dr. Mengele shouted. Immediately, the orchestra director ordered her to leave the stage. Without hesitation, I took over and performed the piece, apparently to the satisfaction of Dr. Mengele who nodded approvingly as did his friends. Later, I learned that my sister had been transferred to another unit within the camp. Despite my pleas that she be allowed to return to the orchestra, she remained there until the commandant ordered everyone to evacuate the camp. The Russians were closing in. We were herded onto a train, along with other prisoners, and taken to the Bergen-Belsen Camp, where I saw my sister again. She'd lost weight and could barely walk. The camp was overcrowded, with overflowing latrines that made us gag and cover our noses. We had little to eat, and only if we shoved our way to kettles of soup that smelled of rotten meat and boiled gizzards. Prisoners died every day. Some from hunger, others from beatings by Nazi guards. It soon became clear that only the fittest would survive. Sadly, my sister perished, less than a week before the British Army liberated the camp." She paused to wipe the tears that ran halfway down her cheek.

The doorbell rang. Maria got up to answer it. "It's probably Joe Spiewak," Mr. Feinberg said. "He lives in Israel and arrived in town a couple of days ago. He wasn't sure he could make it, but I'm glad he did."

Maria soon returned, accompanied by a gray-haired man dressed in a rumpled brown suit. He sat next to her. Mr. Eisenberg gave him a moment, then asked, "Would you like to share your story?"

The man glanced around. "I came to Tucson to visit an old friend from Poland, and it was he who suggested that I speak to you." He hesitated. "I'm not very good at expressing myself, especially before a group of strangers."

"We understand." Mr. Eisenberg nodded.

"When I and other Jews arrived at the Sobibor camp, in June of 1942, the first thing the Nazis did was to separate those who had specialized skills. I was a jeweler. Others were carpenters, blacksmiths and tailors. We soon learned that our particular skills had saved us from being killed. Unlike other camps, prisoners were not used as slave workers in plants or factories. Sobibor was designed for the sole purpose of killing Jews. Our job was to sift through the prisoners' personal belongings. Jewelry, gold and other valuables were removed and placed in boxes. In time, we became accustomed to seeing cattle cars filled with Jews, arriving at all hours of the day and night. Those deemed to be of no value were immediately removed, stripped naked, and taken to the gas chambers, which the Nazis sadistically called the *Road to Heaven*.

"By the summer of 1943, we heard rumors that Sobibor would be closed. If true, the Germans would have no reason to keep us alive. We had to try to escape. Within days, we came up with a bold and dangerous plan…to kill every German guard and SS officer. But we needed a leader, someone who knew how to kill. Alexander Stronski, a former soldier, was the perfect choice. Over the next few weeks, we held secret meetings to discuss what each of us had to do. I'd been a jeweler most of my life and didn't know if I could actually do it, kill a man in cold blood. But I did. On the day Alexander gave the order, I lured an SS officer to my space to show him a special gold piece that I had removed from one of the prisoners. When he picked it up to examine it, I stepped to the side, grabbed a knife and stabbed him. He lunged at me and I stabbed him again.

"By this time, all the prisoners were out of their barracks. Though we'd killed most of the guards, the soldiers manning the towers fired upon the prisoners trying to get to the gate. Months later, I learned that out of six hundred prisoners, less than half made it safely out of the camp and into the forest. Sadly, most were recaptured. Only fifty-eight prisoners, including myself, remained free for the rest of the war. The camp was later dismantled and never reopened." He sighed, softly. "They say time is a healer. But for me…I still have a long way to go."

After a moment, Mr. Feinberg turned to Mr. Cohen. "Would you like to share your story?"

"I was fourteen years old," he began slowly, "when German soldiers ordered all Jews in our village out of their homes and into the street. We didn't know what was happening. The women, including my mother and sister, cried as soldiers forced them into trucks. Suddenly, my mother yelled 'run David, run.' I saw the fear in her eyes, pleading for me to run, and so I did. A soldier went after me but gave up when I jumped over a fence. I kept running until I got to the woods, and only then did I stop to rest. But not for long. I knew I had to keep going. Hours later, I stopped for the night. The next day, I looked around and felt safe enough to build a hiding place so no one could find me.

"For the next few days, I ventured out, hoping to find other Jews.

I saw none until I heard the sound of a machine gun firing, some distance away. Curious, I walked toward the site to get a better look. From a few yards away, I saw a group of Jews, three men and two women, lying dead near a smoldering fire. Afraid someone would see me, I backed away, slowly. I stopped when I heard faint cries coming from behind a bush, near a stream. I glanced around, then rushed toward the stream. I could hardly believe it. Someone, perhaps the mother, had left a baby under a pile of branches. I hurried to take the baby and some provisions back to my hiding place.

"For two days, I cared for the baby as best I could. It cried constantly, and I knew I would have to leave my hiding place to look for someone to help me. The next morning, I packed up what I could and set out further into the woods. Miraculously, I stumbled upon a young Jewish couple who had been out there for over a week. The woman took the baby and promised to look after it. I could have stayed with them, but I knew there were partisans living in the woods, and I wanted to join them. I never found them. As luck would have it, I ran into a group of Russian soldiers. They were preparing to march into German-held towns. They allowed me to join them. When the war ended, I searched for my mother and sister and discovered they had perished in Auschwitz. I also found out that the couple who took the baby survived, but the infant had not." He looked away for a second. "When I close my eyes, I can still hear my mother yelling, run David, run."

"Thank you," Mr. Feinberg said. He turned to Mr. Karp. "Can you tell us your story?" He gave him a moment.

"My story begins on a cattle car where dozens of Jews—men, women and children—were forced to ride for three days. There were two buckets, one with water and the other for use as a toilet, to be passed from one person to another. The stench was unbearable. I was positioned in the corner, next to a young woman who couldn't stop crying. I consoled her as best I could, assuring her that everything would turn out all right. You'll see, I said. We'll soon be in a camp where we'll have plenty of food and clean-living conditions. She smiled a little and stopped crying. Her name was Ruth, a nurse from the town of Slovakia. Her parents and two sisters had been taken away on a different train. We continued to talk about ourselves, our families and many other things. By the end of the day, we'd formed a bond that lasted until we reached our destination: Auschwitz.

"Getting off the train, we were met by German soldiers, barking dogs and SS officers who shouted commands to get into separate lines, either to the left or to the right. When a soldier attempted to remove a crying infant from a mother's arm, the woman resisted. 'Please don't take my baby, please don't take my baby,' she pleaded. Unmoved, an SS officer pulled out his pistol and shot them both. Stunned, all we could do was look away and cry.

"While many went to their deaths that day, little did we know that Ruth and I would be spared because of our professions—she a nurse and I, a tailor. Ruth was assigned to an infirmary, where, as part of her job, she had the freedom to walk through the camp. As the camp's tailor, I, too, enjoyed privileges not afforded to others. But not for a moment, did they let me forget that I was a prisoner, subject to being killed for any reason. The highlight of my day was seeing Ruth making her rounds. We soon found a hidden area where we could talk, kiss and sometimes do more than kiss. We were in love and lived for the moment. When we heard rumors about the war coming to an end, we made a pact, that if we survived, we would find each other and marry. Soon after, I learned that Ruth had been transported to another camp. I immediately feared the worst. Within days of Germany's surrender, I wasted no time combing through lists of survivors posted on bulletin boards in towns and villages throughout Poland. For weeks and months, I continued to search for her."

He bowed his head and paused. "It's been over twenty years, now, and I'm not giving up. I'm determined to find out what happened to her. I'd heard about Mr. Feinberg…how he had assisted others in finding their loved ones, and so I drove all the way from Prescott to speak to him about Ruth. It was his idea that I speak before this group."

"Thank you," Mr. Feinberg said. "In the morning the Center will send out a locator request to our friends in Israel and Europe. Hopefully, by the next time we meet we'll have some good news to report." He looked at Mr. Weiss. "Would you like to share your story?"

"I am the last one to speak, so I'll try to be brief."

"Take as much time as you need."

"Very well." He took a second to collect his thoughts. "Before the war, my wife and I and our two daughters lived in a village south of Warsaw. We led a quiet, simple life. When the Germans arrived, everything changed. They wasted no time rounding up Jews and forcing them into a ghetto in Warsaw—sealed off by fortified walls and barbed wire. Guards were posted all around the perimeter. No one was allowed to leave, not even to buy food or medicines. The Germans' plan was simple: starve us to death. The sick and the elderly were the most affected, and they died within weeks. We had to fend for ourselves, as best we could. Young men soon found a way to sneak out through the sewage tunnels or over sections of unfinished walls. They brought back food and much needed supplies. By this time, hundreds of Jews had been taken away or died of hunger.

"It became clear that we had to do something...something that would show the Germans that we were prepared to die as honorable men and women, rather than go to our deaths like lambs to the slaughter. We would resist, to the last man or woman, if necessary. From that point on, we quietly went about acquiring guns and explosives, smuggled in from the Aryan side. We also built bunkers where people, including my wife and daughters, could hide. When German soldiers entered the ghetto, to load Jews into trucks as they had been doing for months, we fired upon them. They quickly retreated. We stood our ground, knowing full well that they would return with heavy artillery. Every time they entered the ghetto, we repelled them, killing dozens of soldiers and disabling their high-powered guns. They regrouped and came back with tanks."

He took a deep breath. "Everything came to a head when a German tank smashed through one of our bunkers, killing over a dozen Jews, including my wife and daughters. I was less than five yards away. All I could do was cry and keep fighting. By this time, we had begun to run out of ammunition. Someone had to leave the ghetto to ask for help from the Polish partisans. I volunteered. Just after midnight, I quietly entered one of the tunnels and made my way to the other side. God was with me as I emerged from the tunnel near a large truck that afforded me cover. There were soldiers nearby, and I waited until they trained their attention to the sound of homemade bombs, meant to explode at that moment. I walked away as fast as I could, down one street and then another. I'd been given a name and address of someone who could take me to the partisans. Within hours, I stood face to face with one of their leaders. We can't last much longer, I pleaded. We need machine guns and ammunition. My words fell on deaf ears as he shook his head. 'With or without our help, you'll not come out of this alive.' When he said this, I realized that he didn't understand. We were fighting, not to save our skins, but for our dignity as human beings, and to show the world that we fought as bravely as any soldier on the field of battle." He swallowed hard and paused.

"In the morning, as I prepared to return to the ghetto, I heard the sound of explosions, one after the other. I rushed into the street. The Germans had begun their final assault, razing building after building, so Jews had nowhere to hide. By the end of the day, the resistance was dead, as were hundreds of men, women and children." He lowered his eyes. "My only regret is that I did not return to die alongside my Jewish brothers and sisters."

A somber mood filled the room until Mr. Feinberg stood and brought the session to an end. "I want to thank all of you for sharing your stories. Just remember, you are not alone."

~ * ~

"I'm glad we came," Helen said, as they got in the car.

"Me too." Bryan shifted into drive and headed back to Helen's house. "It was an eye-opener. I'd heard survivors' stories before, but not like this. The emotions that ran through me ranged from shock to anger. How could the Germans, who were among the most enlightened people in Europe, allow this to happen?" He shook his head. "I never thought I'd say this, but maybe the JFJ is justifiably right."

"The JFJ?"

"Jews for Justice. It's an underground Jewish group dedicated to finding and assassinating Nazi war criminals in South America and other places, including the U.S. O'Hara told me all about it."

She turned to him with a puzzled look. "I've never heard of them."

"Most people haven't. I think they'd like to keep it that way."

Helen hesitated. "About Mr. Feinberg's idea for a book about Holocaust survivors…is that something you'd want to do?"

He half-shrugged. "Maybe, but you can't work on two projects at the same time. We'll see." Not until he stopped for a light, did he spot a gray Volvo in his rearview mirror. The light turned green, and he pressed the accelerator. The Volvo followed, staying at least three car lengths behind.

Minutes later, he dropped Helen off at her house and headed back to his place. The Volvo stayed back but was still in sight. When he slowed to pull into a 7-Eleven, the car barreled past him. He breathed a momentary sigh of relief.

Chapter Twelve

When the phone rang, Bryan turned off the shower, grabbed the nearest towel and rushed to answer it.

"Have you had any visitors?" O'Hara asked in his usual, brusque manner.

"What are you talking about?" With his hand, Bryan brushed away the beads of water over his eyes.

"Someone broke into my condo yesterday morning while I was out playing golf."

"Did they take anything?"

"Not what they were looking for, the fucking bastards."

"You mean your list of Nazis?"

"After your visit, I thought something like this might happen, so I put it in a safe place, away from here. They won't give up, you know. That's why I called to give you a heads up."

"I'm glad you did. Last night, a gray Volvo followed me for several miles, and now I know why. That's not all, someone left an anonymous note in my mailbox. Short and to the point, it said: *Stop your investigation or face the consequences*."

A heavy sigh. "These guys are *contractor*s and that's what worries me. They have no loyalties, not even to themselves. They'll stop at nothing, not even murder—to get what they want. So, heed the warning and don't give them a reason, more than you already have, to go after you. Right now, they're more worried about me and what I might do…like go to the press. But I'm saving that for later when I know it can do some good. Hate to cut this short, but I'm expecting a call from my doctor." He hung up,

Bryan dried himself off and got dressed. Maybe O'Hara was right. He should heed the warning about the *contractors*. Right now, they had no reason to come after him, and he wanted to keep it that way.

Later, Bryan got a call from Elizabeth, Mrs. Muller's daughter, wanting to confirm what her mother had told her. "Is it true? Will my brother and I receive part of my stepfather's estate?"

"It's true, all right. His attorney should be calling you soon to explain what you need to do."

"It all came as a shock. Just so you know, I loved my stepfather and felt closer to him than to my mother. At the time, my best friend was Eva Levi, a Jewish girl who was born in a displaced persons' camp in Europe. I learned a lot about her and her family, most of whom died in the camps. So, when my mother told me about my stepfather's Nazi past, I wanted nothing more to do with him, and I told him so."

"Did your mother tell you why I went to see her?"

"She said you were working on a book about ex-Nazis, like my stepfather. She mentioned something about a deathbed confession."

"I showed her a copy of it. Your stepfather had dictated it to his nurse moments before he passed."

"Will you include it in your book?"

"Probably. But it won't be finished for at least another year. By the way, are you still friends with Eva? The reason I ask is because I'm thinking about writing a separate book about Holocaust survivors and their families."

"I lost contact with her a few years ago—don't remember why exactly—but I can try to reach out to her if you want. It'll give me an excuse to rekindle our friendship."

"Great. Let me know if you have any luck."

"About your book…can you call me when it's published?"

He smiled. "I'll do more than that. I'll send you an autographed copy."

~ * ~

Bryan didn't expect to hear from Elizabeth for at least a couple of days. He was surprised when she called three hours later. "I located my friend, Eva. With the help of a mutual friend I found out she and her mother had moved to Raleigh, North Carolina. We had a long talk and caught up on each other's lives. When I brought up your name and the book you were writing, she said she'd be willing to talk to you. The problem is, she has no plans to return to Phoenix anytime soon."

He sighed. "And I have no plans to travel to North Carolina. But thanks for trying."

"She did offer to write her story, which I thought was a good idea. When she finishes, she'll mail it to me and then I'll forward it to you."

"Sounds good. I can't wait to read it."

~ * ~

"I'm so glad you could make it," Sylvia said from across the table in the middle of the restaurant. "We should do this more often." She dipped her chip in the salsa and took a bite.

"Yes, we should." Helen nodded. "To be honest, your call came at a good time. A lot has happened since we last spoke." Brief pause. "Bryan's Nazi research has turned into an obsession, which I really don't understand. The good thing is that he's found a new interest: Holocaust survivors. We recently attended a meeting where we listened to their stories. Mr. Feinberg, the man who runs the group, suggested that Bryan write a book about their experiences. If he agrees, which I think he will, I'd like to help in whatever way I can."

"So...you'll be seeing more of each other." She smiled. "Any chance you'll change your mind about...well, you know what I mean."

Helen sipped her margarita. "You're as bad as Bryan's grandmother. He introduced me to her. From the moment we met, she was convinced we were a perfect match, despite Bryan's insistence that we were just friends."

"Just friends," Sylvia repeated. "Well, if it were me, I'd at least test the waters, so to speak."

Helen grinned. "That makes me wonder. Were you and Bryan ever—?"

"I'm surprised he never brought it up. If you want to know the truth, we dated for a while. Nothing came of it. We were polar opposites."

"I'm glad you told me. Not that it makes any difference, considering that I'm not interested in a relationship with him or anyone else."

Sylvia gave a skeptical smile. "If you say so."

Helen changed the subject. "Let's order." She signaled the waitress, coming out of the kitchen. "They make the best *chili con carne*. You should try it."

Chapter Thirteen

Phoenix

Sitting in a booth toward the back of the bar, a nameless man in a dark, flannel suit checked his watch: 5:15 p.m. He sipped his drink. Seconds later, a tall blonde, with a cool demeanor, appeared and sat across from him.

"Right on time." The man downed the last of his watered-down Scotch. "Bring me up to date…and it better be good."

The woman looked around as though to make sure no one listened. "We searched O'Hara's place from top to bottom. No list, no nothing."

"What about Bryan De Luca?"

"He's an unwanted nuisance. We've been tailing him for a while, just to see what he's up to. If O'Hara gave him the list, it could be anywhere. He and Helen Darby, the nurse who cared for Mr. Muller, met with a group of Holocaust survivors. As far as we know, the people who attended have nothing to do with O'Hara or his list."

The man shook his head. "I don't like what I'm hearing. If the names should fall into the wrong hands, a lot of heads will roll, including yours and mine. Do what you have to do but *find that list*." He picked up his empty glass and set it back down. "Do I make myself clear?"

"Perfectly."

"If there's nothing more to discuss…" He signaled the waitress to bring him another Scotch.

"Enjoy your drink." She flashed a fake smile as she stood and walked out of the bar.

~ * ~

The next day, Bryan got a call from Mr. Feinberg. "Remember Mrs. Goldberg, the woman from the survivor's meeting?"

"What about her?"

"Well, just a few minutes ago, she called and said she was ready to tell her story. I mentioned your name and asked if she would mind talking to you. Surprisingly, she had no objections. Are you interested?"

"Yes." He nodded. "Since we last spoke, I've decided to take you up on your suggestion...to write a book about survivors and their experiences. So, I'm glad you called."

"Great. You can meet her here at my place...say, in about an hour?"

"I'll be there," Bryan said, and hung up.

~ * ~

Mrs. Goldman never showed.

"Let's give her a few more minutes," Mr. Feinberg said. "By the way...the other night, at Maria's house, after everyone had left, Mr. Spiewak returned, wearing a pair of thick-lensed glasses that he'd left in the car. He wanted to look at the photograph of the young girl again. For almost a minute, we watched as he studied it under an overhead light. Finally, he smiled and said that he knew her: Sofia Stern, from Krakow, Poland. Sofia was a friend and classmate of Spiewak's youngest daughter, Elsa. He confirmed that the Nazis had arrested Sofia and her parents in the middle of the night. They were never seen or heard from again."

An audible sigh. "Mr. Adelman would've been pleased to know that after all these years, someone finally put a name to the face on the photograph." Mr. Feinberg waited a second, then got up and dialed Mrs. Goldberg's number. No answer.

"Do you have her address?"

The man scribbled it on a piece of paper and handed it to Bryan. "Let me know if you have any luck."

Minutes later, Bryan pulled into a convenience store. He dialed Helen. "Glad I caught you," he said when she answered. "I'm on the way to meet Mrs. Goldberg, the Holocaust survivor who wasn't ready to tell her story. Want to come along?"

"I was about to leave to run an errand, but it can wait. Can you pick me up?"

"Sure. See you in twenty minutes."

Chapter Fourteen

When Bryan and Helen strode up to Mrs. Goldberg's mid-town house, Bryan halfway expected that she would refuse to talk to them. To his surprise, she invited them into her home. They sat around a coffee table cluttered with discount flyers and grocery coupons.

"I want to apologize for not showing up for our meeting. I don't know why, but at the last minute, I panicked. I should have called, but..."

"I understand." He gave a sympathetic smile. "We still want to hear what you have to say."

The woman took a slow breath. "Very well. I'll tell you my story. My family lived in Amsterdam where my parents owned a bakery shop. I worked there most days, usually in the morning. When the Germans invaded the country, our everyday lives were not affected, at least for the first few months. It was not unusual for German soldiers to come into the shop. One day, a young man about my age or a little older, came in and ordered coffee and a strudel. His name was Victor, and he sat at a table next to a window. Over the next few days, he showed up and I could tell that he liked me. So, it came as no surprise when he asked me out. I liked him too, and I said yes. The next day we met at the park and from there we went to the cinema showing a Hollywood movie. For the next two months, we met at the park almost every day. Despite our religious differences, we had much in common: he played the cello, I played the piano. We both loved poetry and going to the theater." She paused and sighed wistfully. "We were in love. It was the happiest time in my life."

She continued. "But things were about to change. The Germans ordered all Jews to wear the Star of David. It made it hard for Victor and me to be seen in public. But we still met at the park in a secluded area where no one would notice. In the short time that we dated, I learned a lot about him and his family." Her lips quivered. "The day it happened...the day we were spotted sitting under a tree, we had talked about running away to Switzerland. Two German soldiers arrested me and took me to a holding area filled with dozens of Jews, mostly women and young girls. I did not see my parents and feared for their safety. The next morning, we were taken to the train station where guards forced us into cattle cars. The train took us to the Ravensbruck camp where I remained for the duration of the war. The conditions were horrible and twice I became so sick that I almost died. What kept me going was the thought that I would see Victor and my family again. When the camp was finally liberated by the Russians, the first thing I did was to look for my parents, who, thank God, had survived. They knew nothing about Victor and me and were shocked when I said that I wanted to find him." She became quiet. "You'll have to give me a moment. It's hard for me to relive the past that continues to haunt me, even to this day."

"Take your time." Bryan nodded.

"Like I said, I wanted to find Victor, and so I travelled to Heidelberg where his family still lived. As you can imagine, his parents were surprised to see me. They were helpful, though not particularly friendly. The war had ended months before, but they had not heard from Victor. All they knew was that he had been sent to the Russian front. Only recently did they learn he had been taken prisoner. I burst into tears. He was alive and that's all that mattered. No one could say when he would be released. I returned to the Netherlands with a heavy heart, but with the hope that he would soon be released.

"About a year later there were rumors that Germany and Russia had reached an agreement for the release of all prisoners. Weeks and months passed, and nothing happened. We almost gave up hope until his parents received word that Victor was seriously ill and that he would be permitted to return to Germany." She closed her eyes for a moment, then reached to wipe the tears that ran down her cheeks. "He died before he could be released."

"I'm sorry," Helen said. Bryan echoed her words.

An awkward silence. "A Jewish girl in love with a German soldier did not sit well with some people, who said hurtful things to me, accusing me of consorting with the enemy, which is totally untrue. Our love was pure and innocent." She sniffled. "I have no regrets, except one: I wish Victor and I had married, which I know would have been difficult under the circumstances."

They chatted with the woman for a few minutes longer, then left and headed back to Helen's house.

"Quite a story," Bryan said. "Any thoughts?"

Helen sighed. "A love story with a sad ending. It's not what I expected. Makes you wonder what would have happened if Victor had survived." Brief pause. "Have you thought anymore about what you're going to do?"

"You mean about documenting survivors' stories?" He nodded. "I'd like to see where it will take me. But I won't be a note taker, which some people find distracting. I'll be a listener. I want the survivors to trust me. Later, when I'm back in my office I'll write everything down, as best as I can recall."

She hesitated. "Do you mind if I tag along on your next interview?"

Bryan smiled. "If you hadn't asked, I would have suggested it. I may miss something, or you might have questions of your own." He glanced at the clock on the dashboard. "Hungry? There's a taco shop up ahead. I stop by there at least once a week. They make their own corn tortillas, daily, just like they do in Sonora."

"Sounds good to me."

After lunch, Bryan dropped Helen off at her house and headed back to his own. Throughout the short drive he kept an eye on his mirrors.

When he walked through the door, he heard the phone ringing. It stopped before he could answer it. Seconds later, it rang again.

"Hello?" he said into the receiver.

"I believe we have something in common," said the caller, a man with a friendly tone to his voice.

Bryan gripped the phone. "Who is this?"

"Let's just say we're on the same side. We know you've been trying to gather information on Nazis criminals in America, and I think I can help."

"I'm listening."

"Go to Sabino Canyon. Walk up the main road till you get to mile

62

marker one. You'll see a picnic table between the road and the creek. Meet me there in one hour. If you don't like what I have to say, you can walk away, and we'll never see each other again."

"If this is some kind of trap…"

"Just be there, and make sure you're not followed." He hung up.

Later, against his better judgment, Bryan grabbed his keys and headed out the door.

Chapter Fifteen

Bryan arrived a few minutes early. Surrounded by mesquite trees, ocotillos and prickly pear cactus, the picnic table sat on a ledge overlooking a creek. He waited almost ten minutes before a man wearing a European style cap and round, wire-rimmed glasses appeared. About fifty, tall, with a tannish complexion, the man walked up from a path that ran parallel to the creek. He introduced himself as Joaquin. "I wasn't sure you'd show up." He glanced around, then took a seat.

"I almost didn't, but I was curious." Bryan stared at him for a second. "You're with the Jews for Justice, aren't you?" he guessed.

"If you've heard of us, then you know that our mission is quite different from other anti-Nazi organizations. But before we get into that, I'd like to get something out of the way…to break the ice, so to speak. Do you know how many Nazis were executed following the Nuremberg trials?"

Bryan gave a small shrug. "I'm embarrassed to say that I don't."

"Would it surprise you that of the thousands of Nazis who committed heinous crimes against Jews and innocent civilians, only *ten* were executed?"

Bryan frowned. "Only ten?"

"It's hard to believe, but it's true. Many fled to South America and some—as you well know—came to America, which brings me to the reason that I called. We know you're in contact with Sam O'Hara who used to work for Immigration in Washington. We also know that O'Hara, who hates Nazis as much as we do, compiled a list of Nazi criminals living in this country. I considered reaching out to him, but decided not to, as it would be too risky. He's being watched, even as we speak. Besides, he might not agree with our objectives."

"You mean…to kill the ex-Nazis."

"We prefer the word *execute*, which is a sentence they would receive if they were sent back to Germany or Israel." He leaned forward. "Look at it this way, we are correcting an injustice that occurred because too many people, including some in this country, were willing to forgive and forget."

Bryan crossed his arms. "Seems to me, you're seeking revenge more than justice."

"Maybe we are. But we're not alone. Most Holocaust victims would have no qualms about killing the Nazis who brutalized them and their families. Unfortunately, the millions who perished at Auschwitz, Dachau, Bergen-Belsen and many other camps lost their voice, and so it is up to us to speak for and act on their behalf. Whether you agree or disagree with our methods, we will not rest until there is not a single Nazi criminal left in the world. It's an ambitious task, but if we don't do it," he took a breath, "nobody will."

"I see where this is heading. You need my help in getting O'Hara's list."

The man nodded. "The government would do anything to protect the names on that list. Sooner or later, they're going to put real pressure on O'Hara. That's why we're asking that you do what you can, before it's too late."

A brief silence. "Even if O'Hara were to give me the list, I'm not sure I would hand it over to you. It's not what you want to hear, and maybe after I leave this meeting, I'll feel different." He shrugged.

"Like I said before, you're free to walk away. If we meet again or if we don't, it's up to you." He handed him a piece of paper with a phone number. Bryan slipped it in his shirt pocket, then got up and walked away. Joaquin remained seated.

A short, slender man who had been watching them from behind a cluster of ocotillos, less than five yards away, soon appeared. He carried a .38 revolver tucked in his waistband.

"Spot anything?" Joaquin said.

The man shook his head. "Not a thing. So, how did it go?"

"Hard to say. I expected it would be an easier sell, considering he's part Jewish." Joaquin paused for a moment. "This project he's working on…to interview Holocaust survivors…maybe we can use it to our advantage."

"What do you mean?"

"Well, what if we were to steer him to survivors who are sympathetic to our cause."

The man smiled. "I like it. I'm sure we can count on Mr. Feinberg to make it look good."

"Get in touch with him and let him know what we have in mind." He glanced around, then led the way back to the main road.

~ * ~

Back home, Bryan called Helen and filled her in on his meeting with Joaquin. When he was through, he said, "I have to admit that part of me admired his commitment to their cause."

"So, how did you leave it?"

"I told him that even if O'Hara gave me the list, I'm not sure I would turn it over to him. He appreciated my honesty, and we said nothing more about it."

"Do you think he'll contact you again?"

He shrugged. "Maybe."

A brief silence. "I…I don't know if I should tell you, but after you dropped me off, I drove to a bookstore on Fourth Avenue. When I came out, I spotted a white Camaro, with two men sitting in it, parked across the street. Later, when I got in my car and drove away, I noticed the same car following me from a distance. By the time I reached my house, it had disappeared."

"I'm not surprised." He hesitated. "Maybe you should keep a low profile to avoid drawing attention to yourself. Whoever sent them may see you as my partner, which makes you a target just like me."

"What are you suggesting? That I not accompany you when you interview survivors?"

"For a while, at least. Later, when things calm down—"

"Look, I appreciate your concern, but I'm not afraid—well maybe a little." She chuckled. "Seriously, I think what you're doing is important, and I'd like to continue being your sidekick."

"Fine with me. But if you change your mind, I'll understand."

"I won't. Just call me."

Chapter Sixteen

Two days later

Bryan called Helen. "Just got off the phone with Mr. Feinberg. He gave me the name of a Holocaust survivor who lives in Willcox. He's expecting me. I can be at your house in twenty minutes."

"I just put a cake in the oven. If you'd called ten minutes earlier…"

"No problem, just call when you're ready."

~ * ~

"Please excuse the mess," Lucas Steiner said, as he greeted Bryan and Helen. He ushered them to the kitchen table that had been cleared off except for a cup of coffee and a folded copy of the local paper. "I moved in four days ago, as you can see…" He gestured toward the living room filled with unopened boxes. "Have a seat."

"I want to thank you for agreeing to see us," Bryan said. "I understand you've not told your story before."

The man nodded. "The reason is that I didn't want anyone to know I am a homosexual. Since my arrival in America, I've kept it a secret. By talking to you, I risk being attacked, verbally and physically. But it's important that you tell my story so that people will know what evil men are capable of doing." He took a sip of his coffee, then moved the cup to the side. "First of all, you should know that I am not Jewish. I came from a wealthy, Austrian family which supported Hitler, at least in the beginning. I hid my homosexuality well. I was discreet and no one, except my older sister, knew about my secret life. She also knew about my affair with Karl, a Jewish man. I was nineteen, he was twenty-one. When the Germans arrived, we had to be extra careful. They were arresting Jews and homosexuals."

The phone rang. "Excuse me." Mr. Steiner got up to answer it. "Yes," he said into the receiver. "They got here a few minutes ago." He nodded. "Okay." More nodding. "I'll talk to you later."

"That was Mr. Feinberg…just wanted to make sure you had arrived." He sat back down and continued. "For our safety—Karl's more than mine—we decided to stay away from each other. Every time I heard about Jews being arrested, I prayed he was not among them. A month passed and then another. I felt safe. Then one day, just before dawn, the authorities knocked at our door. They came to arrest me. My father protested, but to no avail. I spent the next three days in a warehouse with other homosexuals who had been arrested the same day. 'Someone betrayed us,' said one of the men. 'I think it was my friend, Albert. Yesterday, I saw him being taken away from his home. He's not here which means that he gave up the names of everyone in this room.'"

Mr. Steiner paused a moment. "On the fourth day, we were transported to the Buchenwald camp. The SS considered us the lowest of the low and regularly beat us or sodomized us with a broom stick. Then they boiled off our testicles with scalding water. Others were used as target practice. As our numbers began to dwindle, I lost hope of ever seeing my parents and sister again. Then, on a sunny day in May, I was ordered to report to the commandant's office. When I walked through the door, I couldn't believe my eyes. There stood my father. 'You're free,' he said. 'Let's go home.' He had paid off a mid-level German official. At the moment, I was overjoyed, but later when I thought about the other prisoners, I felt guilty. They did not have a rich father to bail them out." He sighed. "Even after all these years, I still think about them."

"What about the ones who were picked up the day you were arrested?" Bryan asked.

"Of the thirty-four men who were arrested and sent to Buchenwald, only two survived. Years later, I found out that it was true…Albert had given our names to the Gestapo. They beat him so badly that he died the next day."

"What about your friend, Karl?" Helen said.

"He and his entire family died at Auschwitz." He swallowed hard, to keep from sniffling. "For years I used to break down and cry whenever I thought of him. But not anymore. My tears have turned to anger. If I knew I could get away with it, I would personally kill every Nazi that escaped justice. They reduced me to a shell of a human being. That's what they did to me."

Bryan and Helen looked at each other. "Well, again, thank you for sharing your story," Bryan said.

"When you write about it… please don't leave anything out. The world should know that we, too, were victims."

~ * ~

Back in the car. "Before, whenever someone mentioned the Holocaust, I immediately thought of the Jews," Helen said. "I had always known that the Nazis arrested thousands of homosexuals, but consciously or unconsciously I never associated them with the Holocaust."

"Come to think of it, I didn't either. When Mr. Feinberg called, he simply gave the man's name and address. I assumed he'd be Jewish. Mr. Steiner is a victim just the same, so I'm glad we got to hear his story."

"Do you think he really meant what he said…that if he could get away with it, he would kill every Nazi that escaped the gallows?"

"He meant it all right. You could tell by the tension in his voice."

Later, as they approached Helen's house, Bryan blurted, "I've decided to interview the two Nazis who worked at Mittelwerk."

She looked at him. "You're not serious. The people who sent you the anonymous note are dangerous. Have you forgotten what they did to the man in Florida?"

"It's a risk I'm willing to take. Someone has to expose them. I don't see anyone else stepping up to the plate." He forced a smile. "If it'll make you feel any better, they'll probably slam the door on my face the moment I introduce myself."

"So, why even try?"

He thought about it for a second. "There's an old saying: better to fail than to regret not trying." He smiled. "Want to come along?'

"Thanks, but no thanks."

He dropped her off at her home. Tomorrow he'd take the first flight to Denver. Josef Bauer's last known address was in nearby Aurora.

Chapter Seventeen

Josef Bauer refused to talk to him. No big surprise. Would Kurt Hofmann be any different? Only one way to find out. The man lived in Seattle. He booked a mid-day flight and arrived there just before midnight.

In the morning, Bryan drove to Hofmann's residence, north of the city. He parked across the street, waited a moment, then got out and strode toward the house. He heard muffled voices coming from inside. When the door opened, a young, dark-haired woman in a nurse's uniform came out. He flashed a quick smile. "Excuse me. I'm a friend of the family. Is everything okay?"

"I'm not allowed to talk about my patients, but…" she hesitated, "maybe your visit will help cheer him up. Don't be surprised if he doesn't recognize you."

"Thanks for letting me know." He didn't count on Kurt Hofmann being ill. For a second, he wanted to turn around and walk back to his car.

The door opened and a middle-aged woman stepped onto the porch. "May I help you? I saw you from the window. Are you here to see my husband?"

Bryan hesitated. "Yes, but—"

"He's not doing well, and he needs his rest. If you don't mind, can you come back another time?"

"Martha," said a voice from inside. "I can't find my slippers. Where are my slippers?"

"I'm sorry. My husband needs me. Come back later, or better yet tomorrow." She closed the door.

Back at the airport, Bryan booked an early flight to Tucson. With time to kill before boarding, he called Helen. "I'm glad I caught you," he said when she answered. "I'm in Seattle…came here to talk to Kurt Hofmann. When I got to his house, a visiting nurse who had just seen him said he probably wouldn't recognize me. I had told her I was a friend." He let out a sigh. "To confront a sick man, possibly suffering from dementia…well, it just didn't seem right. So, I turned around and left."

"What about Josef Bauer?"

"He shut the door in my face."

"In a way, I'm glad you didn't talk to them. You gave it your best shot, and I have to give you credit for that." She hesitated. "When you get back, I've got something to tell you. Nothing serious, but I'd rather do it in person."

"Can you give me a hint?"

She chuckled. "I'd rather not. Why don't we meet tomorrow at the coffee shop near my house, say around nine?"

"I'll be there." He checked his watch. If he hurried, he had just enough time to grab something to eat.

Chapter Eighteen

"Yesterday, when we spoke on the phone, you sounded a bit mysterious." Bryan emptied a packet of sugar into his cup. "If it's about a Holocaust survivor—"

"That's not it." She smiled. "I went to see your grandmother. She got my name from the sign-in registry at the nursing home. I have a listed phone number. She called and asked if I could drop by. We had a lovely visit."

He stirred his coffee and took a sip. "So, what did you talk about?"

"Mostly girl talk. You would've been bored if you'd been a fly on the wall."

"That's it?"

Helen blushed. "Well, she did ask if I had any feelings for you."

"What did you say?" He grinned.

"I was honest and said that I really didn't know you that well. Then, I changed the subject."

"Good answer. She's a sly one, so don't be surprised if she brings it up again."

Helen sipped her cappuccino. "So, tell me more about your trip."

"There's not much to tell. What I said yesterday pretty much sums up what happened, or rather what didn't happen. I'm disappointed of course, but" he lifted his shoulders, "what else could I have done? Anyway, I'm back, ready to work on our project."

"Our project," she said, smiling. "I like the sound of that."

~ * ~

Back home, Bryan answered a call from O'Hara. "Looks like someone we know got what they deserved," he said.

"What happened?"

"Josef Bauer and Kurt Hofmann are dead. They were shot in their homes, which if I had to guess, was the work of the JFJ."

Bryan's mind raced back to his meeting with Joaquin. "Oh, my God! They must have followed me when I went to see them."

"What are you talking about?"

"I met with their leader, a guy named Joaquin. They knew about your list of Nazis and wanted me to help them. I didn't immediately say no, which they took as a sign that I might change my mind."

A heavy sigh. "Well, don't be surprised if the guys in black show up at your door. For sure, they'll be knocking on mine."

"So, what should we do?" Bryan said, a frightened tone in his voice.

"Just go about your business as if nothing happened. If confronted, play dumb even if they threaten you with arrest and imprisonment for violating a bullshit law that no one has heard of. And whatever else you do, do not, I repeat, do not contact Joaquin or anyone from the JFJ. One more thing—"

The doorbell rang and it startled him. "Hold on…don't hang up." Maybe it's *them.* He hesitated, then crossed the room and peered out the window. Nothing. He opened the door.

"Would you like to buy some candy?" said a young, freckled-faced boy carrying a box filled with chocolate bars. "It's for our baseball team…to buy new uniforms."

Bryan smiled. "Sure," he said, relief in his voice. He handed him a five-dollar bill for a couple of bars.

Chapter Nineteen

Phoenix

The nameless man and the blonde operative sat in a booth toward the back of the bar. They were there to discuss the killing of Josef Bauer and Kurt Hofmann.

"According to the cops in Denver and Seattle, a white male in his early thirties had visited each of the victim's homes hours before they were killed," said the blonde. "A sketch artist's rendition of the man matched the face of…are you ready for this? Bryan De Luca."

He frowned. "Was he involved?"

"If you mean with the killings…probably not. My guess is that he was followed when he went to their homes. We believe the JFJ may have tried to recruit him. Regardless, they knew that sooner or later, he would eventually lead them to Bauer and Hofmann, and possibly others."

"So, what do you propose that we do?"

"We can approach De Luca and scare the crap out of him. Maybe show him the picture drawn by the artist. We'll lay it out for him. It's us or the local police who already assume he was part of the team that made the hit."

He thought about it for a moment. "I have a better idea. Why don't we let him sweat? Scared people tend to make mistakes. Give it a few days. Let's see what he does."

She nodded. "We'll stay on him twenty-four seven."

The man released a slow, steady sigh. "I'm getting a lot of heat from above. The killing of Bauer and Hofmann changes everything. The JFJ is not going to stop until they get O'Hara's list. He's a cagey old fox who thinks he's got us over a barrel."

"Well, doesn't he? If you want my opinion…"

"Save it. I know what has to be done." He reached for his drink and took a quick gulp.

~ * ~

Still reeling from O'Hara's phone call, Bryan grabbed his keys and headed out the door. He needed someone to talk to.

"Sorry for not calling," he said, when Helen opened the door. "You were right. I should have left well enough alone." He followed her to the couch. "I let my guard down and they took advantage of it."

"They?" she said with a puzzled look.

"The JFJ. They followed me all the way to Denver and then to Seattle. Josef Bauer and Kurt Hofmann were killed shortly afterwards."

"Oh, my God!" Her eyes opened wide. "So, what are you going to do?"

Bryan shook his head. "I don't know. O'Hara suggested that I go about my business as if nothing had happened, which to be honest, will be hard to do."

"I think he's right. Talking to another survivor will help, don't you think?"

"Maybe. In the meantime, I need to prepare myself for the possibility that so-called government contractors might soon be knocking at my door. By now, they've pieced things together and made up their minds that I was in on it, that I led the killers to Bauer and Hofmann."

"You don't know that." She shook her head.

"No, I don't. And I don't know what the police in Denver and Seattle are doing." He sighed. "I thought about calling them to explain that I tried to talk to them and that I had nothing to do with their murders."

"When you went to see them, did you identify yourself to anyone?"

"I didn't get a chance. Still, people saw me and that's what worries me."

"Well, the way I see it, you'll probably make things worse by coming forward. Your explanation would raise some eyebrows, especially when you have to admit that you actually met with the leader of the JFJ."

Bryan released a quick sigh. "You make a lot of sense." He gave a weak smile. "You're a good listener, Helen." He stood, then crossed the room to the window facing the street. Through semi-closed blinds he looked for surveillance. He saw none and turned around. "I should be going. I've taken enough of your time."

"What's the rush? It's almost lunchtime. I could heat up some leftover pasta Bolognese and make a quick salad."

He thought about it for a second. "Sure, why not."

"It's homemade, by the way. My neighbor is from Northern Italy, and a couple of days ago she brought over enough for at least four people."

The impromptu lunch had taken Bryan's mind off his troubles, for a while at least. He left Helen's house in a better mood, which faded when a gray Volvo appeared in his rearview mirror.

Chapter Twenty

In the morning, Bryan went through his mail. The letter from Elizabeth, Mr. Muller's stepdaughter, finally arrived.

Dear Mr. De Luca,

Enclosed is a summary of Eva's story based on conversations she had with her mother, Sarah Levi. They plan to move back to Arizona later this year or the next. I'll keep you posted.

Sincerely,

Elizabeth Muller

Dear Mr. De Luca,

My name is Eva Levi. I was born in a displaced person's camp in Austria where my mother, who was three months pregnant, was forced to live after the war. While there, she met a Jewish-American soldier. A friendship soon developed. Months later, he proposed to her, and they were married shortly afterwards. I was eight months old at the time. Later, my adoptive father arranged for all of us to move to his hometown in Arizona, just north of Phoenix.

When I was twelve, my mother sat me down and told me that my stepfather was not my real father. She explained as best as she could, the circumstances of her pregnancy when she was a slave worker in a Nazi-run factory. Of course, none of this mattered to me because I considered my stepfather to be my true father. He and I were very close, and it hurt me deeply when he died in a motorcycle accident almost three years ago.

Not until I entered high school, did my mother share her story about her life in Poland, when the Germans rounded up every Jew in her village. She was sent to a prison camp and never saw her parents again. Because she was strong and healthy, she was moved from one work camp to another. Throughout her captivity, she saw many of her co-workers die from beatings or sheer exhaustion. And because she was young and pretty,

*soldiers frequently took her aside. They raped her and laughed as if it were
a game. She got used to it, thinking and praying all the time that if she
could survive another day, another month, she might live to see her family.
She had no way of knowing that her parents and most of her relatives had
perished in Auschwitz. She has happy memories of her life in Poland
before the Germans arrived, and she would like to return someday to the
village where she was born and raised. But she fears that her neighbors
will shun her, just as they did on that fateful day when she and her parents
were led away by the Nazis.*

*I've provided only a glimpse into my mother's life during the war.
She's not told her entire story to anyone and looks forward to meeting you.*

Cordially,

Eva Levi

~ * ~

Mr. Feinberg called two days later. "David Faber, a Treblinka
survivor wants to tell his story, but only on the condition that his true name
remain confidential."

"Not a problem," Bryan said. "When can I see him?" He took
down all the necessary information. The man lived in Yuma, Arizona.

Later, Bryan dialed Helen's number. He repeated what Mr.
Feinberg had said about David Faber. "His call couldn't have come at a
better time. The trip will do me good. I know we'll be followed, but that's
okay. At least they'll know I'm not afraid."

The next day, Bryan and Helen drove to Yuma, about a three-and-
a-half-hour drive on I-8. Mr. Faber lived in an assisted living facility on
the edge of town. From a distance, it looked like a modern, two-story
apartment complex, complete with a mini-golf course and an oversized
pool next to a gazebo.

"We're here to see David Faber…he's expecting us," Bryan said
to a woman from across the information desk. She looked Hispanic, mid
to late fifties, and wore a white uniform with a name tag over her right
breast pocket that said Olivia.

She flipped through a roster. "He's in room two-twenty-one, but you won't find him there. I saw him walk out just a few minutes ago. He likes to sit in the patio, next to the gazebo. It's to your left as you exit the building."

"Thank you." Bryan smiled. They walked back out. Just as the woman had said, Mr. Faber sat in a weathered-looking chair in the patio, reading a book.

"Mr. Faber?" Bryan said.

The man nodded. "You must be Bryan De Luca."

Bryan shook his hand, as did Helen.

"We can talk here or inside if you prefer," Mr. Faber said.

Bryan glanced around. "It's a beautiful day. Here is fine." They grabbed a couple of chairs and sat across from him."

"Before we begin, I want to make sure you will not use my real name in whatever you plan to write. If you have a problem with this—"

"I completely understand. I give you my word that your name will remain confidential."

"Good. Now let me tell you about Treblinka and the day the prisoners revolted." He drew a quick breath. "On that day in August, which is forever etched in my mind, several prisoners broke into the arsenal and took rifles, handguns and grenades. They set buildings ablaze and killed many guards. But the Germans had machine guns, and within minutes killed over a hundred prisoners. Still, at least two hundred, I among them, managed to escape. Some took to the roads, others to the forest. The Germans went after us and killed or captured most of the escapees. Only about seventy made it to freedom.

"I ran through the forest and lost all sense of direction. When I heard dogs barking, I kept running on adrenaline mostly. I ran for miles until I reached a clearing. In the middle was a farmhouse. If I knocked on the door would the farmer help me or turn me in? I didn't know what to do. By that time, I was exhausted and wanted only to rest for an hour or two. As I debated whether to take a chance with the farmer, a jeep with four German soldiers appeared. They jumped out, searched the house and barn and left as quickly as they had arrived.

"I waited several minutes, then dashed across the field. With my heart in my throat, I banged on the door. Help me, please help me, I shouted. I looked around and knocked again.

"'Go away,' said a man's voice from inside. 'We don't want any trouble.'

'It's our Christian duty,' said a woman's high-pitched voice. 'We have to help him.'

"A moment passed and then the door opened." 'Get inside before someone sees you,' the farmer said. Mr. Faber released a steady sigh. "They took me in, fed me, clothed me and protected me until the end of the war. Sadly, others were not so fortunate. Perhaps out of fear, prejudice or both, many Polish citizens alerted the Germans. I am forever grateful to the Polish family who risked their lives to save a Jew like me. Yes, many Poles turned their backs on us, but just as many did the right thing, which makes them heroes in my book."

"Are you in contact with any of the prisoners who escaped?" Bryan asked.

Before the man could answer, a young man dressed in green scrubs appeared. "Mr. Faber, I'm sorry to interrupt. If you want to go to the park, the bus will arrive in ten minutes."

"Thank you, but my daughter will be picking me up a little later." He waited for him to walk away. "To answer your question, I've not kept up with anyone. Most just wanted to put it all behind them. I heard that a few took their own lives, some recently. I think we all shared a sense of guilt because we survived and so many didn't. My hope in talking to you, is that ordinary people who read my story will support the courageous efforts of underground Nazi hunters like…" He glanced around as though to make sure no one listened. "Like the JFJ."

Bryan and Helen looked at each other. "I've heard of them," Bryan said.

"Then you know what they do and why they instill fear in Nazis hiding among us." He clenched his jaw. "If I were younger, stronger, I would gladly join them."

Helen hesitated. "Is there a reason why you don't want your name to be revealed?"

The question seemed to upset him. "I did not intend to speak of it," he said tersely. "But maybe if I explain what happened just before the start of the revolt, you'll understand." He took a slow breath. "The truth is, I was scared and hid behind a barracks. The others were so brave, and all I could do was cower and pray that I not be killed that day. When I saw a group running toward the exit gate I joined them. I took advantage of the chaos around me. That is not how I want to be remembered, especially by my children." He paused, then quietly said, "There were many heroes that day. I was not one of them."

Mr. Faber had nothing more to add. After the interview, he got up shook hands and walked away. Bryan and Helen waited a moment, then crossed the lawn to the parking lot.

Later, on the road to Tucson, Bryan checked his mirrors. "Don't look now, but there's a black Mercury that's been tailing us since we left Yuma. Funny that I didn't spot it on the way down here. No matter. All we did was interview another survivor. If they want to check it out, fine with me." He shrugged. "So, what was your impression of Mr. Faber?"

"He surprised me. First, when he admitted that he had no part in the actual revolt and then when he mentioned the JFJ. No other survivor has mentioned them before,"

"You're right. Makes me wonder if he said it just to see our reaction."

"About his request that you not use his real name…how are you going to handle it?"

Bryan looked at her. "I'm not sure. Maybe I'll say something to the effect that his identity is being protected for personal reasons. Then I'll use a pseudonym…or I might just use the pseudonym and offer no explanation. I'll think about it and decide later. I've got plenty of time."

They arrived in Tucson three hours later. He dropped Helen off at her house, then drove himself to his own. The black Mercury was still tailing.

It was beginning to get to him…not knowing when or if they'd knock on his door. In a way, he wished they would just get it over with.

Chapter Twenty-One

Bryan got his wish. The following day, the blonde operative and a tall, brutish-looking man appeared at his door. The man produced a 9mm pistol and pointed it at him.

"I've been expecting you," Bryan said, releasing a nervous sigh. His eyes fixed on the gun; he allowed them to enter.

"Then you know why we're here," said the woman. They sat across from him in the living room. "Let's talk about what happened in Denver and Seattle." She handed him a copy of the police sketch of an unidentified male.

Bryan studied it for a second, then gave it back to her. "I know how it looks, but I had nothing to do with their murders. I went there to interview them about my project on former Nazis living in America. Someone...someone must have followed me. That's the absolute truth."

"We believe you, but I'm not sure the cops will. They're looking for you as we speak." She sounded calm, almost friendly until she grabbed the gun from the man and pointed it at Bryan's head. "No more games. Either you tell us what really happened, or I pull the trigger."

Tiny beads of perspiration formed over Bryan's brow. "All right...I'll tell you what you want to know." He took a second to gather his thoughts. "About a week ago, I got a call from a man who knew I was doing research on Nazi criminals in America. He offered to help, and so I agreed to a meeting. His name is Joaquin." Bryan repeated what the man said and when he was through, admitted that he sympathized with their cause, but not with their methods. "I made it clear that even if O'Hara were to give me his file, I could not in good conscience turn it over to him."

"Have you talked to him since?"

Bryan shook his head. "When I heard about Josef Bauer and Kurt Hofmann, I was tempted to call him, but I didn't." He reached into his wallet and retrieved a small piece paper with Joaquin's phone number scribbled across it. He handed it to her.

She looked at it, then gave it to her associate. "Check it out."

The man got up, crossed the room to a kitchen extension and dialed. "It's been disconnected." He hung up and returned to the couch.

"I'll give it to you straight," said the woman. "We need to find O'Hara's list of Nazis before the JFJ does. Like it or not, you're in the middle of a situation that will test you in ways that you never imagined. Your only option is to work with us or face the consequences, which I assure you will not be pleasant." She turned to her associate who looked like he wanted an excuse—any excuse—to beat the crap out of him.

Bryan blinked twice. "What-what do you want me to do?"

"Let's start with the JFJ. I have no doubt that Joaquin will reach out to you again, so stay alert." She jotted a phone number on a small card and handed it to him. "Don't lose it. When you talk to him, let him think that you remain sympathetic to their cause, which is true, right? What we want is for him to arrange another meeting. Any questions?"

"No," he said, barely audible.

She paused, then glanced around and instructed her associate to search the place. "Take your time, Bruno. We're in no hurry." She leaned forward. "Now, tell me about O'Hara."

Bryan slumped in his seat and released a quick sigh. "I met him only once at his home in San Diego. He was very open with me and offered to help in whatever way he could. I never saw his list of Nazis, though he referred to it when I asked about Josef Bauer and Kurt Hofmann." The phone rang and it startled him. "I'm expecting a call from my grandmother's doctor. She's got a heart condition."

"Let it ring," she said.

Bryan continued. He held nothing back as he repeated everything O'Hara had said during subsequent phone calls. When he finished, he let out a sigh. "He trusts me, but not enough to give me his list. Besides, he knows you're keeping tabs on me."

The woman stared at him. "Look, I know you see us as the bad guys, but the fact is, we have a new enemy: the Soviets and their network of spies. No one cares about the Nazis anymore. Recruiting them after the war made sense. The Russians were doing the same thing. Believe it or not, they hired more Nazis than we did." She paused. "Whether you agree with me or not doesn't really matter. We have a job to do, which brings me to a question that you should consider carefully before answering. Do you think O'Hara will go to the press?"

"I don't know." Bryan shrugged. "Maybe."

"Which is it?" she said, leaning closer.

He considered the question. "I think he would, but only as a last resort."

Moments later, Bruno returned to the living room. "Nothing." He shook his head.

"By the way…a bounty of one million dollars has just been placed on Joaquin's head. He's not Jewish, you know, but he picked the wrong side." She and Bruno looked at each other, then got up to leave. "You'll be hearing from us. In the meantime, don't do anything stupid."

Bryan's jaw muscles twitched uncontrollably.

"Aren't you going to see us out?" she said, a mischievous tone to her voice.

Bryan stood and walked ahead of them. Almost at the door, Bruno clenched his fist and slammed it into Bryan's stomach, doubling him over. He dropped to the floor, writhing in pain.

"Have a nice day." The man chuckled as he opened and closed the door behind him.

Seconds later, the phone rang. Out of breath and still hurting, Bryan struggled to get to the phone. "Hello," he answered, exhaling through his mouth. He hoped it'd be his grandmother's doctor.

"You okay?"

He recognized Helen's voice. "I had some unexpected visitors," he said in between shallow breaths. "Can you come over? I'll tell you all about it." He gave her the address.

When Helen arrived, the door was partially opened. "Come on in," Bryan called from inside. He sat on the couch with his head against the back cushion.

She scanned the room: books and papers strewn across the floor, pictures pulled from the walls, cushions thrown about. "What happened?"

She took a seat next to him.

Bryan sat up. "A woman and a man with a gun, possibly the ones who've been tailing me, showed up at my door. They were all business and handed me a police sketch of the man seen at Bauer and Hofmann's homes, hours before they were killed. Before they left, the man punched me right in the gut." He winced as he clutched his stomach.

Her eyes widened. "Are they working with the police?"

"No, but they threatened to call them, if I refused to cooperate." He repeated everything the woman said and the questions she asked. "Of course, they're more interested in O'Hara's list than anything else. As you can see, they made sure I wasn't holding out on them."

"So, what are you going to do?"

He shook his head and sighed simultaneously. "There's not much I *can* do. I thought about calling O'Hara, but I'd have to admit I betrayed his trust." He got up, crossed his arms, and began to pace. "These guys are pros, which means that they won't give up until they get what they want. There's no telling what they'll do next. Right now, I feel like a pawn in a chess game." He stopped pacing and sat back down.

"What about the survivor's project? You do want to continue, don't you?"

He nodded, forcing a weak smile. "It's a good distraction. Maybe I'll call Mr. Feinberg for another lead." He glanced around. "Want to help me clean up the mess?"

"Sure, then we can go out to lunch, and I'll tell you why I called." She smiled. "My treat."

"Fine with me."

~ * ~

The blonde operative stepped into the nearest phone booth and dialed a number she knew from memory. "We just left De Luca's place. It didn't take much to get him to talk. He admitted that Joaquin tried to recruit him."

"What about O'Hara?" said an impatient sounding voice.

"He confirmed what we suspected…that O'Hara is playing his

cards close to his chest. Whoever he gave his list to is anybody's guess. We searched De Luca's place and found nothing."

A heavy sigh. "I want you to stay on him. We're running out of time. If nothing develops, and I mean soon, then you'll have to do what we discussed. Don't let me down." He hung up.

The woman left the booth and joined her partner, sitting in the car. "We'll stay on De Luca a while longer," she said. "Only this time, he won't know we're around."

Chapter Twenty-Two

"So, what is it you want to tell me?" Bryan said, after the waitress delivered the menus.

"This morning, I happened to be at the main library when I overheard a man who walked with the aid of a crutch, inquire about a certain book on Buchenwald. Naturally, my ears perked up. A staff member suggested that he sit at a table while she checked to see if they had it. She returned momentarily with the book, which she placed in front of him. I waited a couple of minutes before I approached him. Are you a Holocaust survivor? I asked. He seemed unsure whether to answer. When I told him about you and your project, he nodded and said he had been a prisoner at Buchenwald. His name is Walter Mendel." She smiled. "He agreed to an interview."

"When, where?"

"Tomorrow at nine at the library. I reserved a private room for one hour."

"What else did he say?"

"Not much, really. Our conversation was brief, and I didn't want to intrude any more than I already had."

He let out a sigh. "Thanks, Helen…for giving me something to look forward to."

~ * ~

Late evening

"I heard you had some visitors," said the caller.

Bryan recognized Joaquin's voice. "How-how did you know?"

"I have my sources. You told them about me, didn't you?"

"I had no choice. They threatened to call the cops in Denver and Seattle. Because of what you did, everyone thinks I'm involved...that I set them up."

"Well, didn't you?" He half-chuckled. "You led us to them. But why dwell on it? Nobody's shedding any tears, not even Tanya, the woman you met. She and I go back a long way when we worked together to help smuggle guns into Israel. Unfortunately, she sold out to the highest bidder, which brings us to where we are today." Brief pause. "You have to decide. It's them or us. Think about it the next time you interview a Holocaust survivor."

"I know what you're trying to do, but—"

"Write this down." He waited for Bryan to grab a pen, then gave a new phone number. "I'll be in touch." The line went dead.

Chapter Twenty-Three

Bryan and Helen sat at the end of a long table in a room she'd reserved at the library. The clock on the wall said: 9:17 a.m.

"Maybe he changed his mind," Bryan said.

"Let's give him another ten minutes."

Moments later, the man appeared. He walked with a cane instead of a crutch. "I would've been on time," he said with a slight German accent, "but I missed my bus and had to wait for another."

Helen smiled. "You're here and that's all that matters." She introduced him to Bryan who shook his hand and waited for him to sit across from them.

"I want to thank you for agreeing to meet with us." Bryan paused. "Helen said you are a Holocaust survivor."

"I'm a Jehovah's Witness and that was my crime." He looked at Helen. "Yesterday, when we met at the library, I was there to check on a new book about Buchenwald. I was curious to see what the author had to say about Ilse Koch, the commandant's wife, who took delight in torturing and abusing prisoners. They called her the *Witch of Buchenwald*."

"What did you find?" Bryan said.

"The book was mostly about her husband, Karl-Otto Koch and the way he ran the camp. Ilse's name appeared in only one section. It detailed her cruelty but made no mention of what she did to prisoners who had prominent or unusual tattoos. I witnessed it firsthand, and it made me sick to my stomach. One day, a young man with a large tattoo of a cobra on his back arrived at the camp. The next morning, he was singled out and taken to a special room next to the commandant's office. Hours later, another prisoner and I were instructed to go in to remove the body. The man had bled to death, the result of his tattoo and surrounding skin being crudely cut from his back."

Helen's brow furrowed. "Why would anyone want to do that?"

"Because Mrs. Koch needed it for her collection. According to a prisoner who had done some odd jobs for her, she kept sections of tattooed skin on a table in the main room of her house. In the corner, atop a roll top desk, sat a small lamp with a shade made from the tattooed skin of one of her victims. After the war, I learned she had been arrested. I immediately sent word to the prosecutors, offering to be a witness against her. They asked for a signed statement from me, and I complied. I never heard back from them, not even after she was found guilty and sentenced to life imprisonment. She later committed suicide in a women's prison in Aichach, Germany."

"Did others know of her sick, little hobby?" Bryan asked.

The man nodded. "I heard from other prisoners that she had done this to at least six other men with distinctive tattoos. And she did it with the approval of her commandant husband, who by the way, was killed by his own men a week before the arrival of American troops." He glanced at the clock on the wall. "I hate to cut this short, but I have another appointment. I must get going."

"I wish we could've talked to him longer," Helen said, after the man had left.

"Me too. He really didn't tell us much about himself. Maybe later we can meet with him again."

"Why do you suppose no one bothered to contact him? His information certainly seemed credible?"

Bryan shrugged. "Maybe they had enough evidence against her and didn't need his testimony, or—what seems more likely—they had no way of corroborating what he observed." He looked at his watch. "Our time's up. Let's get out of here."

~ * ~

Mid-afternoon

"My name is Martha Faber," the caller said, her tone somber. "I'm David Faber's daughter and I thought you should know....my father passed away early this morning. He'd been ill for some time."

The image of him in the nursing home in Yuma, flashed through Bryan's mind. "I'm sorry," he said, softly.

"Yesterday, before he went into a coma, he talked about your visit. He said I was to let you know that he had changed his mind—he wanted you to use his real name in your project. He never talked about his experiences, so I'm glad you were able to speak to him. I wished he had done it sooner."

Bryan closed his eyes for a second. "Thank you for letting me know." He jotted down funeral details, then quietly said goodbye.

Chapter Twenty-Four

The phone rang, just after 8:00 a.m.

"Quick. Turn on the TV…channel 9," Helen said.

Bryan put the receiver down and turned on the set.

BREAKING NEWS

"We're standing in front of a home in Aurora, Colorado, where three days ago, an intruder inexplicably killed the owner, Josef Bauer," said the reporter, a tall, slender man with a trace of a Brooklyn accent. "The motive remained a mystery until today when our news hotline received an anonymous call, presumably from the killer, saying that Josef Bauer was a former Nazi who had escaped the gallows by emigrating to America."

From the corner of his eye, the reporter spotted the man's wife coming out of the house and he rushed toward her. "Ma'am, is it true that your husband was a Nazi?"

"He was a fine, decent man who loved America and its people," she said as she hurried toward a waiting cab. "Please, no more questions."

The reporter then turned to a neighbor, a gray-haired woman, standing next to a flowering hedge. He shoved the microphone in her face. "Do you believe what's being said about Mr. Bauer?"

She started to shrug. "I've lived next to him and his wife for over ten years, and to tell you the truth, I barely know them. They kept to themselves…weren't very sociable, him more than her. I knew he was German, which didn't really bother me. I mean, the war was over, and we all did our best to move on, some more than others." She clutched a small, silver Star of David that hung around her neck. "If you'll excuse me, I must go inside."

The reporter continued. "Earlier today, we checked with investigators working the case, and so far their only lead is a well-dressed, white male in his early thirties who was seen visiting Mr. Bauer's house, hours before the murder. They have extended their search by alerting and distributing a composite sketch of the man to police departments across the country. When asked if they knew Mr. Bauer was a former Nazi, as the anonymous caller had suggested, they declined to comment. In the meantime, viewers are asked to call police if they know or have seen the man in question. For the moment, he is considered a person of interest." A police sketch of the individual flashed across the screen, along with a 1-800 number.

Bryan turned off the set and picked up the phone. "This is turning into a nightmare. The worst part is that there's not much I can do about it." He let out a sigh.

"I agree. That's why you can't let it get you down. When this blows over—which I'm sure it will—if only because the press will move on to other stories, you should think about taking a break from all this."

Bryan nodded. "I think you're right. It'll do me good to get away for a few days."

The doorbell rang in the background. "Hold on," Helen said. She returned, momentarily. "Someone left a newspaper clipping of the sketch shown on TV and a note with the words, *Anyone you know?* scribbled in red ink. "This is insane. What are they trying to do?"

"Send you a not too subtle message that my fate is in their hands, meaning Tanya and her friends."

"Tanya?"

"I didn't tell you, but Joaquin called the day we met for lunch. He'd found out that the blonde operative, whom he called Tanya, had paid me a visit. He knew her from before when they were on the same team, so to speak. He made it clear that sooner or later I'd have to pick a side: him or her." Brief pause. "Before I forget, Mr. Faber's daughter called to let me know her father had passed. She said that before he went into a coma her father requested that she call me. He'd changed his mind and wanted me to use his real name."

"I'm glad you told me. Now, I wish we had talked to him longer."

"Me too." He sighed. "Before you called, I had planned to visit my grandmother. She's not doing well. Want to come along? I'm sure she'd love to see you."

"Sure. Just give me half an hour."

~ * ~

One of the male caregiver's recognized Bryan as he stepped in the door. "You just missed her," he said, rushing his words. "Your grandmother suffered a stroke and had difficulty breathing. An ambulance took her to the hospital on Grant."

By the time Bryan and Helen arrived at the hospital, the woman had died. "I talked to her on the phone just yesterday," Bryan said, in numb disbelief. "She sounded weak but in good spirits." He paused. "I have to notify her rabbi and make arrangements."

Later, at Helen's place, she handed him a brandy and sat beside him.

"It's been a tough day. I'm glad you came with me." Bryan sipped his drink. "Her funeral is the day after tomorrow. It would mean a lot to me if—"

"I'll be there." She gave a reassuring smile. "And if you need help later today or tomorrow, all you have to do is ask. Your grandmother was a lovely woman. We hit it off right from the start. I only wish I had known her earlier."

Bryan stayed only long enough to finish his drink. He'd made an appointment with his grandmother's Rabbi and left the house less than a half hour later.

Chapter Twenty-Five

"You okay?" Helen said, after the last of the mourners had left.

Bryan nodded. "I had a good meeting with Rabbi Hirsch. Afterwards, I felt a calm that made it easier for me to accept my grandmother's passing. We prayed and talked for almost an hour. He was surprised that I knew so little about the Jewish faith—considering I'm half Jewish—and so we talked about that, as well. For reasons that were never clear to me, my mother rarely talked about her Jewish background. She stopped practicing her faith about a year or two before she married my father. She passed almost four years ago and I regret that we never had a real conversation about it.

"Rabbi Hirsch asked if I would be open to learning more about Judaism. He even offered to be my personal teacher." Bryan poured himself a glass of wine and took a sip. "He kind of put me on the spot, and so I said OKAY. Now, I wish I'd held off before committing myself."

"I'm sure he meant well." Brief pause. "I wouldn't mind knowing more about Judaism myself. I mean…why not?"

"Really?" He stared at her for a second.

She nodded. "The truth is that up until a few weeks ago, I knew little to nothing about Judaism. Sure, I had some Jewish classmates in college, but we ran in different circles, and I never gave it another thought, until now."

A quiet pause. "If Rabbi Hirsch agrees, you're welcome to join me,"

Helen smiled. "Just let me know when and where."

"By the way, late yesterday I got a call from Mr. Feinberg. He told me that he had just received a documentary film titled *Death Mills*. It was produced shortly after the war to educate the German populace about crimes and atrocities committed by the Nazi regime. Unbelievably, many

Germans refused to believe that Hitler had condoned the killing of Jews throughout Europe. He invited us to a screening tomorrow at an activities center near Armory Park. Most survivors have declined to attend, which I can understand."

"I think we should go."

Bryan nodded. The doorbell rang. "Excuse me. I'll see who it is."

He opened the door. "I hope I'm not too late." Mr. Feinberg extended his hand. "I was at the hospital visiting an old friend and lost track of time."

"Please, come in." Bryan led the way to the living room. After an exchange of pleasantries, Helen excused herself. She motioned for them to remain seated. "I'll see myself out."

Later, Bryan called Helen. "Mr. Feinberg just left. I'm glad he dropped by. We had a good talk, and just before leaving, he said he'd found another survivor. Her name is Johanna Lieberman, a survivor of Ravensbruck. Unlike other camps, it was exclusively for women. The problem is that she lives in Mexico City. She's an activist and a writer. He learned about her through a mutual friend in Tucson. He promised to let me know when she's back in town."

"Did he say whether she would be willing to talk to us?"

"He thinks she would. Apparently, she has been very open about her experiences and has written a couple of articles, one of which praised the work of anti-Nazi groups like the JFJ."

"Sounds like a strong woman who's not afraid to speak her mind. I can't wait to meet her."

"I'll keep you posted. About tomorrow…the screening starts at three in the afternoon. I'll pick you up thirty to forty minutes earlier."

"Great. See you then."

Chapter Twenty-Six

Bryan and Helen sat next to Mr. Feinberg in the first row, facing an oversized screen. At exactly 3:00 p.m. Mr. Feinberg stood and faced the audience.

"Thank you all for coming." He looked across rows of people. Most were middle-aged or older, though a few were college age and younger. "The film you are about to see was produced in 1945 by a Jewish Hollywood director, whose mother, stepfather and grandmother perished at Auschwitz. They were among the six million Jews that were killed by the Nazis in death camps throughout Germany and in occupied territories. I should warn you that the images are graphic." He waited a moment, as though to allow anyone who wished to leave to do so, then returned to his seat.

The film began with civilians at Gardelegen, Germany being forced to carry 11,000 wooden crosses to the site where an equal number of concentration prisoners were killed by the SS. They had been herded into a large barn and burned alive, hours before the arrival of Allied troops. Next came scenes from the camps: huge crematoriums and piles of corpses hastily left by retreating Germans, dazed survivors—little more than flesh covered skeletons wandering about, mass graves filled with the bodies of men, women and children. Miraculously, six women were found alive, though just barely, among corpses that had been thrown into a ditch.

Orchestral music played in the background, which at times seemed inappropriate or too loud. Whatever the intent, it added little to the somber mood of the film.

Frame after frame of the hour-long documentary depicted the callousness with which Nazi guards beat, starved and ultimately killed most of the prisoners. They collected and sold their hair, jewelry, and gold teeth that had been removed from their mouths. Nothing was wasted. Not even their charred remains from the crematoriums. They were ground and sold to local farmers for fertilizer.

It was all too much for an elderly couple sitting in the second row. They quietly got up and walked out. Soon, others joined them. When the film ended, no one spoke, not even Mr. Feinberg. Like mourners leaving a funeral, some sobbed or walked with heads bowed as they made their way to the door.

Back in the car, Bryan shook his head. "I just can't get the images out of my mind. War is one thing, but cruelty and barbarism is another. The Germans were Christians—many of them Catholics—so the question is why? Why did the most enlightened people of Europe abandon their spiritual faith…their sense of morality?"

"If you don't mind, I'd rather not talk about it," Helen said, softly. She closed her eyes and leaned back on the head rest.

Later, as they pulled into her driveway, she reached for his arm. "Want to come in?"

He looked at her for a second. "You sure?"

She nodded and gave a weak smile. "I'll pour us a drink."

Helen carried two wine-filled glasses, handed one to Bryan, then sat beside him. "I'm still trying to process what we saw. More than once, I was tempted to look away, but I couldn't. It was like watching a bad horror movie." She took a long sip of her wine.

"What bothered me most was the last few minutes of the film when they showed a German officer being interviewed. He was arrogant and unrepentant…just like the Nazis who stood trial at Nuremberg. 'I was just following orders,' he kept repeating."

"Makes you wonder if he had a wife and children. Surely, he must have been a good man, a good father, before the war."

Bryan sipped his wine. "Well, you can put the blame on Hitler, but it would be too easy. At some point, Germans will have to come to terms with the fact that not all of their fathers and grandfathers were guiltless, and for reasons that had nothing to do with Hitler."

~ * ~

Mr. Feinberg called just before 10:00 p.m. "We didn't get a chance to talk after the screening. Everyone left so quickly."

"Can you blame them?" Bryan said, a bitter tone to his voice. "It was a visual nightmare, an abomination of good and evil turned upside down."

"I agree. That's why more people should see it. I've arranged another screening a week from today. If you can help spread the word…"

Bryan nodded. "Of course. Maybe you should put something in the paper or community flyer."

"Good idea." He cleared his throat. "There's another reason I called. Johanna Lieberman, the survivor of Ravensbruck who lives in Mexico City, is coming to Tucson in a couple of days. I talked to her on the phone. She wants to meet you. She'll be staying with a friend for a few days."

Bryan grabbed a pen and jotted down the friend's name and phone number.

"One more thing…she would prefer to meet with you alone. She was very adamant about it."

A brief silence. "I understand." It was late and Bryan was in no mood to tell Helen that she wouldn't be sitting in on the interview.

Chapter Twenty-Seven

The next day, Bryan dialed Helen. He repeated what Mr. Feinberg had said about Lieberman's visit. "I really wanted you to be in on this one, but he was rather adamant that—"

"It's all right. I'm sure you'll do a great job without me. Speaking of jobs, a position just opened up in the hospital nursery. I had to make a quick decision, so I agreed to take it."

"When will you start?"

"The day after tomorrow." Brief pause. "I'm going to miss being your sidekick."

He smiled. "We made a good team, didn't we? Let's stay in touch…maybe meet for coffee or whatever. That is, if you can fit it into your schedule."

"I'd like that. You can fill me in on everything you're doing. By the way, I'll be on the night shift, which I kind of expected. I hate having to sleep during the day, especially if it's bright and sunny." She hesitated. "I don't know if I should mention it, but I had a bad dream last night. It was so vivid I couldn't go back to sleep."

"Was it about the screening?"

"The entire film was disturbing, but oddly enough only one image stayed with me: a baby with its eyes wide open that had been thrown into a pit filled with lifeless bodies. I had a fitful night's sleep as the image played in my mind over and over again."

A quiet sigh. "I think we all had bad dreams. We wouldn't be normal if we didn't."

~ * ~

From a pay phone next to a pawn shop, Tanya dialed a number.

"Any progress?" said the voice on the other end.

"Nothing, which means De Luca is playing it cool or he doesn't know shit about O'Hara and the list."

An audible sigh. "We've wasted enough time. You know what to do. Call me when you have the list."

"What about Joaquin and the JFJ? Maybe we should…"

He hung up before she could finish the sentence.

Chapter Twenty-Eight

Two days later

"Forgive me for staring, but you don't look old enough to be a survivor." Bryan sat across from Johanna Lieberman in the home that belonged to her friend, Rita Bianco.

A soft, seductive smile crossed Johanna's face. "Should I take it as a compliment?"

Bryan ignored the question. "Who's the artist?" he said, his eyes fixed on a wall covered with paintings of camp prisoners and survivors.

"Rita. Over the years, she's compiled dozens of Holocaust stories and turned them into images that are meant to shock…and yes, make you angry that so many Nazis escaped justice, and no one did anything about it. We're kindred spirits, you might say. You should meet her and talk about your project. Unfortunately, she had to leave for a showing in Sedona. She'll be back in a couple of days."

"Is she a survivor?"

"She's not, nor is she Jewish. Her work is exclusively Holocaust related, though she will occasionally paint a portrait of a friend or family member." She smiled, pointing to a painting on the opposite wall. "It was done some time ago when my hair was much longer."

Bryan looked at her and then the portrait. "You haven't changed much."

"You're being kind." She chuckled, then became serious. "What did Mr. Feinberg tell you about me?"

"Nothing. Just that you were a survivor of Ravensbruck."

She clasped her hands together. "My story is perhaps different from others because I was born in Ravensbruck. My mother was seven months pregnant when she arrived at the camp. What little I know about her is what I learned years later from a fellow prisoner; a woman named Josefina who helped with the delivery. My mother was sent to the gas chambers afterwards, along with other prisoners. I would have been killed as well if it hadn't been for one of the guards. Her name was Heidi. She managed to keep me alive at the risk of her own life. I was three months old when the Russians appeared and liberated the camp. From there, I was taken to a displaced persons camp. A couple from Hungary took care of me for almost a year. Later, I was adopted by an American couple from Pittsburgh. I had a normal life up until I entered high school. My parents divorced, and our lives were never the same. I've had a strained relationship with them ever since."

"What about your birth father?"

"All I know is that he was sent to another camp. His name never appeared on any lists, which means that he probably died. Still, I hold out hope that he's alive and trying to find me." She blinked, causing a tear to run down the side of his face. "I'm sorry, I get emotional every time I think about it."

He gave her a moment.

"Like I said, mine is not the usual survivor story. To be honest, I never had a particular desire to learn about Ravensbruck or the Holocaust. It wasn't until I enrolled in a history class, taught by a camp survivor, that I developed an interest in the Holocaust and its aftermath." She sighed. "Sadly, it is a topic that has been largely ignored, especially in this country."

"I couldn't agree more." Brief pause. "By the way, I'm still looking for more people to interview, so if you know of other survivors…" He produced a business card and handed it to her.

"Now it's my turn." She flashed a small, flirty smile. "Tell me about your project. Do you mind?"

"Not at all. The original idea was to gather information about Nazi criminals who fled Germany after the war." He glossed over the details surrounding the deaths of at least one potential witness and the two ex-Nazis killed by the JFJ. "Actually, it was Mr. Feinberg who encouraged me to interview survivors. When I'm done, I'd like to write a book. It won't be anytime soon, though. I still have many more survivors to interview."

"I think what you're doing is vitally important. We only just met, but if there's any way I can help, besides finding survivors to interview, let me know."

He nodded. "Thanks, I'll keep it in mind."

~ * ~

Mid-afternoon

"I have an idea for your project," said the caller.

Bryan recognized Johanna's soft, silky voice.

"I know it's short notice, but why don't we meet for dinner, and I'll tell you all about it."

"Sure. Just give me the time and place."

"Here, at Rita's. It'll give me a chance to try a new recipe. Would eight be too late?"

He smiled. "Not at all, see you then."

Chapter Twenty-Nine

Bryan arrived at Rita Bianco's home five minutes early. A wooden, hand-painted sign above the doorway said: *Casa Bianco Bienvenidos.* He rang the bell.

"Come on in," Johanna shouted above the sound of the radio playing a Mexican bolero. He stepped inside and waited for her to turn down the volume.

"Have a seat while I make us a couple of margaritas." She smiled.

"It's been a while since I've had one." He sat on the couch, facing the wall covered with Rita's paintings. "How long have you lived in Mexico City?"

"A little over a year. I love it. I rent an apartment not far from the Frida Kahlo Museum, which I visit often. She's the reason I moved there. I'm doing research for my master's thesis on her. Did you know that in addition to being an artist, she was a terrific cook? I made one of her favorite recipes. Hope you like it."

She carried the margaritas into the living room, handed one to Bryan and sat next to him. "*Salud*," she said, raising her glass.

"*Salud*." Bryan took a sip. "Best margarita I've had in a long time."

"I got the recipe from a bartender who used to work at the Kentucky Club in Juarez, Mexico. That's where it was invented."

He took another sip, then set his glass down. "Earlier you asked what Mr. Feinberg had said about you." He smiled. "Now, I'd like to know what he said about me."

"Only that you were part Jewish. Is that why you took on this project?"

"Not really. I was raised Catholic. Even though my mother was Jewish, I knew very little about her faith. She was a lapsed Jew, if that's the right word, even before she met and married my father."

They talked until they finished their drinks, then got up and moved to the dining room. "You can pour the wine, if you'd like," she said, stepping into the kitchen. "It's a cabernet sauvignon from one the oldest wineries in Mexico."

"Sure." He reached for the opened bottle and poured a little into two glasses.

A moment later Johanna brought out a large platter of mixed greens and vegetables and placed it on the table. "It's called a Christmas salad, a Frida Kahlo original." She sat across from him.

Bryan studied the colorful dish: chopped peanuts, sprinkled over slices of jicama, oranges, and beets, with a side dish of ripe tomatoes stuffed with *cotija* cheese. "Looks…delicious," he said, trying to be polite.

"I forgot to tell you…I'm a vegetarian." She smiled.

Bryan filled his plate with a little of everything. He took a bite and then another. "Very good, especially the beets." He sipped his wine. "About your idea for the project…"

"What I had in mind was to include pictures of the camps when Allied forces arrived to liberate them. Maybe put them in the middle of the book or at the end, along with the numbers of prisoners who died at each camp. The images, of course, would be shocking, but that's the point. People need to see the hellish conditions from which less than five percent of all prisoners managed to survive."

He nodded. "I like it. It's a good idea."

They talked while they ate and when they were done, they moved to the couch. The banter turned light, almost playful, then stopped altogether. Sensing a mutual attraction, Bryan leaned over and gave her a peck on the lips. She opened her mouth wider, inviting a deeper, longer kiss.

Moments later, they looked at each other's disheveled appearance and laughed. Their moment of passion had been fast and intense. They put their clothes back on.

Still breathing hard, she leaned back on the couch. "Why don't you pour us a drink?"

Bryan smiled. "You read my mind." He got up, crossed the room to the table and returned with two wine-filled glasses.

Johanna took a quick sip. "Just so you know, I'm not an impulsive person by nature, especially with someone I met only hours before." She smiled. "But it's what Frida would've done. She was a free spirit, just like me."

"Well, then, to your inner Frida." He lifted his glass and waited for her to do the same.

A long silence. "Can I ask you something?" she said, a tentative tone to her voice. "What do you think of the JFJ…Jews for Justice?"

Caught off guard, Bryan paused a moment. "I've heard of them, but I really don't know that much about them," he said, unconvincingly. He picked up his glass and took a long sip.

"Well, the reason I asked is because a couple of months ago, I got a call from an old friend from my college days. He'd read one of my articles in which I defended anti-Nazi groups like the JFJ. He had some *friends* who needed my help, he said. Then he got to the point, rather quickly. Would I be willing to assist in a covert surveillance of a Nazi fugitive flying to South America, with a layover in Mexico City? Of course, I knew what they meant to do.

"I didn't immediately respond, and he asked again, adding that the Nazi had murdered over ten thousand Jews in Poland. Feeling pressured, I said yes. As it turned out the man landed in Vera Cruz. By the time we got there, his plane had already left, bound for Argentina. I breathed a sigh of relief. I've not told this to anyone, so please keep it to yourself."

He nodded. "Of course."

She sat up. "If you were me, what would you have done?"

Bryan thought about it. "Given your background…what you and your mother went through, I might have done the same thing."

"I'm sorry, I didn't mean to put you on the spot."

"That's okay. I've asked myself a similar question. More than once, I might add."

After a moment, Johanna glanced at her watch. "It's getting late, and I have an early flight to Los Angeles, then to Mexico City." She smiled. "But I'll be back in two and a half weeks to celebrate Rita's birthday."

Bryan's face broke into a grin. "It'll give me something to look forward to." He got up slowly and waited for her to walk him to the door.

~ * ~

"He just left," Johanna said into the phone.
"How did it go?" Joaquin said.
"Everything went according to plan. I think he'll come around."
"Good. You can fill me in when we meet."
They hung up, simultaneously.

Chapter Thirty

San Diego

Tanya stepped into a public phone booth and dialed a number. No answer. She waited a couple of minutes, then tried again.

"Tell me you have O'Hara's list," said a familiar sounding voice.

"We grabbed him and took him to a house in the woods. My men worked him over for almost an hour. Just when he started to talk, he made a gasping sound. He needed his pills, he said, then he slumped in his chair and stopped breathing. He must've had a bad ticker. If he hadn't died, we would've—"

"Save it. You failed and now we have to live with the consequences. For your sake and mine, you'd better pray that whoever he gave the list to will keep it till we're old and gray."

"Well, praying never got me anywhere, so unless you have any objections, I'll stay with it a while longer. My gut tells me that De Luca is the key, and he may not even know it. We'll keep an eye on him, at least until I'm sure that my intuition was wrong."

~ * ~

"Am I calling at a bad time?" Bryan said into the phone. The clock on the desk said: 9:00 a.m.

Helen stifled a yawn. "As a matter of fact, I was about to get into bed. But a few more minutes won't make any difference. So, how did it go…your meeting with Johanna?"

"I wish you'd been there. She was a survivor, all right, but her story was different because…are you ready for this? She was *born* in Ravensbruck, just months before the Russians liberated the camp." He repeated everything Lieberman said but made no mention of the dinner they shared. "She's the first real activist that I've met. Her friend Rita is an accomplished artist who specializes in Holocaust art, if that's the right word."

"Sounds like I missed a good interview." She sighed. "I wish I could tell you when or if I'll be able to get back to being your partner. For the next few weeks, I'll be busier than ever. So, if you call and get no answer, you'll know that I'm either sleeping or working. Right now, I'm going through an adjustment period trying to learn new protocols and procedures. But I love my new job, though it'll be a while before I can take an extended vacation."

He nodded. "Well, I know you have to crash. Call me when you think you can get away, even if it's just for coffee and a bagel."

Her face lingered in his mind, moments after he'd said goodbye. Was it because he missed her as a friend and partner, or was it something else? He smiled as he considered the latter.

~ * ~

The phone rang just before midnight. Half-asleep, Bryan let it ring a couple more times before answering it. "Hello?" Dead silence. "Hello?"

"I think something happened to O'Hara," said a man with a nervous tone to his voice.

"Who is this?"

"I'm a friend of his and I haven't been able to reach him. Before he went missing, he gave me your name and phone number. He said I could trust you...that you would understand."

"If you're concerned about his safety you should go to the police."

"He gave me the list," the man blurted.

"Look, I don't know you and we should keep it that way. For your safety and mine, do not tell me anything more. If I sound harsh it's because—"

"Sorry I bothered you," the man said, and hung up.

Had he done the right thing by cutting him off? He wondered, and he wondered if he'd ever hear from him again. He let out a sigh and just lay there, unable to fall back asleep.

Chapter Thirty-One

In the morning, Bryan couldn't get last night's caller out of his mind. The man had reason to be concerned, and he wished he hadn't been so abrupt with him.

Later, when the phone rang, he hoped it'd be O'Hara's friend. It was Mr. Feinberg. "I just spoke with a woman named Anna Lewinsky," he said. "She's not a survivor, but she has an incredible story to tell…about her cousin who died at Auschwitz under unusual circumstances. I think you'll want to hear what she has to say."

Bryan needed the distraction. "Hold on." He grabbed a pen and jotted down the woman's phone number and address. "I'll call her now." He hung up and dialed the number. They agreed to meet at her home in the Foothills.

Thirty-five minutes later he strode up to her ground level condo that had a door knocker in the shape of a hand. It also had a doorbell, which he rang twice.

Soon, a bespectacled forty-something woman appeared. "Please come in." She led the way to the patio. "I love sitting out here, especially on a beautiful day like today." They sat across from each other in matching wicker chairs.

"Can I offer you some lemonade or a soft drink?"

He smiled. "I'm fine, thanks." Brief pause. "I'm curious to hear about your cousin. Mr. Feinberg mentioned that she had died under *unusual circumstances*. What did you mean by that?"

"Her name was Ruth. She was sixteen years old when she and her parents arrived at Auschwitz. Like everyone else, they were herded into a shower room, which as you know became a death trap when toxic fumes began to seep from above. Everyone quickly perished, except Ruth. When the Sonderkommandos—Jewish prisoners that assisted the Nazis—

entered the room, they found Ruth unconscious, but still alive. She survived only because others fell on top of her and shielded her from the lethal gas. The Sonderkommandos acted quickly and moved her to one of their barracks. They summoned the camp doctor to try to revive her, which he did. He, too, was a prisoner and risked his own life by agreeing to help."

"It's a remarkable story. But how do you know that it's true?" Bryan said, a hint of skepticism in his voice.

"After the war, my family settled in Israel. That's where I first learned about Ruth—from an Auschwitz survivor. It was later confirmed when the doctor, himself, mentioned it in a book that he wrote. Despite being forced to assist Dr. Joseph Mengele in autopsying bodies, he was a brave, decent man. I know that many Jews do not see it that way, but he had no choice, really. Just like the Sonderkommandos.

"What happened next is the saddest part of the story." She choked up. "When the camp commandant found out that a female prisoner had survived, he ordered that she be shot. Shortly after, the Sonderkommandos who helped her were also shot. The camp doctor was spared only because he was too valuable to be killed."

A long silence, then she added. "I know how this must sound, but it would've been better if she had died the day she arrived."

Bryan nodded, but didn't say anything.

"May I ask a favor?" She paused. "When you write about Ruth, can you mention that she was a gifted harpist? My mother, who played for the Warsaw Symphony, was her teacher. Her dream was to be a concert harpist. From the time she was six, she impressed everyone with her musical abilities. No one doubted that she would grow up to be a professional musician. My hope is that people will remember her, not just as a victim of the Holocaust, but as a sweet, young woman who loved life as much as she loved her family."

"I promise I'll write about her just like you said." He hesitated. "If you don't mind, can you tell me about your own family?"

She removed her glasses, then put them back on. "Shortly after the Germans invaded Poland, my father began talking about leaving the country. His brother, Ruth's father, was an optimist, believing that the Germans would respect all law-abiding citizens, including the Jews. My father, of course, disagreed and the two argued for days. Shortly after, we left Poland and eventually settled in Portugal. By the time my uncle realized he'd made a mistake by staying, it was too late. He, his wife and my cousin Ruth were arrested and sent to Auschwitz. We stayed in Portugal until the end of the war. Later, my mother was invited to join the Israel Philharmonic Orchestra. We were ecstatic and left Europe within days."

"How long have you lived in America?"

"Three years. I came here to teach a course in ancient languages at the university. My parents are still in Israel. I miss them, but Tucson is home now." She smiled.

Bryan left shortly afterwards. When he got home, he couldn't get something Anna had said about Ruth out of his mind: *It would have been better if she had died the day she arrived.* The more he thought about it, the more he understood why the Sonderkommandos, and the doctor brought her back to life, if only briefly. She got to live another day…that's all that mattered.

Chapter Thirty-Two

Bryan didn't hear about it until he saw it on the morning news. "Late yesterday afternoon, a man who identified himself only as a concerned citizen called police to request a wellness check at the San Diego condo residence of Sam O'Hara," said the reporter, a young Latina dressed in a powder blue pantsuit. "With the help of the manager of the complex, police entered the apartment home where the fifty-two-year-old man lived alone. They found no sign of O'Hara. For now, the authorities are treating it as a missing person's case and request that anyone with information about Mr. O'Hara or his whereabouts call the police or the FBI.

"The case is significant because Mr. O'Hara, a former Immigration investigator, had resigned in protest over the government's post war policy with regard to German immigrants. According to an article that appeared in a Washington Journal, Mr. O'Hara had complained about the flagrant violation of immigration laws by German nationals who entered the country with the knowledge and approval of U.S. Intelligence agencies. At the time, it was feared that he would go public with what officials described as unfounded allegations, but he never did."

Bryan turned off the TV. Seconds later, the phone rang.

"Did you see the news?" Helen said, the second he answered. "My jaw dropped when the reporter mentioned O'Hara's name."

"I'm not surprised. I got a call the night before yesterday from a friend of his who said that he hadn't been able to reach him. He thought something might've happened to him." He sighed. "I told him to call the police. Then he blurts that he had O'Hara's list. He hung up on me after I said I didn't want to hear it."

"Well, it looks like he took your advice about calling the police. You think O'Hara is still alive?"

"I don't know." He shook his head. "My guess is that Tanya and her associates kidnapped him and forced him to talk. Something must've gone wrong, otherwise we would have heard from him by now."

"So, what next?"

"We sit and wait. That's about all we can do." He hesitated. "I know you're busier than ever, but can we get together for coffee or maybe dinner, if you have the time?"

"I'd like that. Give me a couple of days and I'll call you."

Smiling, Bryan said goodbye and hung up.

The phone rang ten minutes later. He answered it on the second ring.

"My name is Bill Taylor," said the caller. "You don't know me, but I'm a friend of Sam O'Hara. His disappearance came as a shock. Right now, I'm at the airport in Boston waiting to board a plane to Los Angeles. I'll have a short layover in Phoenix, and I'd very much like to meet you."

"How did you get my name?" Bryan said, a suspicious tone to his voice.

"I'm a freelance journalist. I'd written an article about a former Nazi living in America that caught O'Hara's attention. He reached out to me, and we stayed in contact ever since. When he resigned from his job, we spoke less frequently. About a week and a half ago, he talked about you and your project. He gave me your number and said I could trust you."

"Give me your flight information."

~ * ~

From across the terminal, Bryan recognized Bill Taylor, who said he'd be wearing a white shirt and blue tie over a pair of khakis. He walked toward him, shook hands, then led the way to a coffee shop. They took a seat in the corner of the room.

"Thanks for coming to meet me," Taylor said. "I know it's a bit of a drive."

"You got my attention when you said you'd written an article about a Nazi living in America."

"It was an interesting case…about a woman named Hermine

Braunsteiner, known as the Stomping Mare of Majdanek.

A smiling waitress appeared and took their order.

Taylor continued. "She got the name because of her cruelty as a Nazi guard at the Majdanek camp. She carried a whip and lashed at prisoners for the fun of it. On one occasion, she whipped a newly arrived toddler and his mother. Then she shot them both on the spot. That alone should have been sufficient to charge her with murder after the war. Surprisingly, no one bothered to do anything. Not even after she emigrated to the United States and married an American citizen. I highlighted her case in an article that I wrote for a small Jewish newspaper. About the only one who showed any interest was Sam O'Hara."

"Did he open an investigation on her?"

"He tried, but at the time, the government really didn't care about prosecuting ex-Nazis, and so the case went nowhere. Then a remarkable thing happened; a stringer for a New York paper, got a tip about Braunsteiner. He confronted her at her home in Queens. Of course, she denied everything. Soon after, he wrote an article detailing her crimes at Majdanek. The government had no choice but to step in and do what they should've done years ago. She's still fighting her extradition to Germany, by the way."

The waitress returned and delivered two coffees. Taylor reached for a cup, took a sip and set it back down.

"Did O'Hara ever mention the list of Nazis who'd been allowed to enter the country?"

"He did. For years he'd been trying to expel them based on the fact they had lied on their immigration applications. Unfortunately, it's probably the motive behind his disappearance. Too many people were after his list."

"Then you know about the so-called *contractors*."

Taylor nodded. "I've heard stories about them."

Bryan sipped his coffee. "Maybe I shouldn't be telling you this, but for some reason, I trust you and I feel that I have to tell someone." He described everything that happened: meeting Helen for the first time, then O'Hara and later, Tanya and Joaquin. When he finished, he let out a sigh. "More recently, I got a call from a man claiming to have O'Hara's list. I told him not to say anything more. That's not what he wanted to hear and hung up."

A small frown crossed the man's face. "You're in a real predicament, that's for sure." He paused. "Have you heard from Tanya or Joaquin?"

Bryan shook his head. "Until we know what really happened to O'Hara and whether or not he gave up his list, there's not much I can do."

Taylor checked his watch. "I wish we had more time, but I have a connection to make." He handed him his card. "Let's stay in touch." He dropped some money on the table, then stood to leave.

They left the coffee shop, shook hands and went their separate ways.

Chapter Thirty-Three

In the morning, Bryan got a call from Johanna's friend, Rita. "We seem to have common interests," she said. "Johanna told me about your project." They talked briefly and agreed to meet at her house around ten.

On the way the over, Bryan thought about Johanna. She didn't seem like the kind of girl who would kiss and tell. Not that it mattered. He smiled, reliving the moment.

When he rang the bell, no one answered. He tried again. "I lost track of time." Rita wore a paint-splattered smock which smelled of turpentine. "I was in my studio. Please come in." She smiled. "Just give me a moment while I change and freshen up."

"Take your time." He stepped inside and crossed the room to the wall covered with Rita's pictures—all done in shades of black and gray, except for a life-like painting of a weeping mother carrying the bloodied body of a young boy. He stared at it for a couple of seconds.

"That was my first Holocaust piece and the only one done in color," Rita said, from behind. "I was in Tel Aviv where I met a woman who told me about her five-year-old son. He had been beaten to death by a German soldier for no reason at all. I spent over two years in Israel meeting and interviewing survivors, many of whom became subjects for my paintings. I used mostly dark colors to show the somber tone that I wanted to convey. As you can see, each one tells a story."

She pointed to a painting of a Jewish Sonderkommando removing the body of his wife from the gas chamber. Next to it, a large rectangular piece showing the terrified look of a man trying to scale an electrified fence at Buchenwald. "It's one of my personal favorites," she said, staring at it.

Bryan crossed his arms. "They say that a picture is worth a thousand words. You certainly proved it."

"Let's sit down." They moved to the couch. "When Johanna told me about your project, I couldn't wait to meet you. What you're doing is vitally important. People, especially in America, are in a slumber when it comes to the Holocaust. They need to be nudged and, in some cases, shaken…to demand that authorities prosecute every Nazi criminal that found refuge in this and other countries."

"I totally agree. If even one Nazi is arrested because of what I uncover, it would have all been worth it." He paused. "I'm curious. What got you interested in Holocaust survivors and their stories?"

She took a second. "When I was in college, I fell in love with a Jewish refugee from Germany. From the beginning, I was fascinated with the stories he told about his family, most of whom died in the camps. We eventually split up, but his stories stayed in my head. So much so, that I decided to make the Holocaust a principal theme in everything that I did. Unfortunately, the subject matter turned off most dealers, even to this day. 'People don't want to be reminded of the horrors of the war' is a phrase I heard over and over again. However, in the last few years my so-called Holocaust art has gained more acceptance. Not a lot, but enough that smaller galleries are requesting to display my paintings, though only one or two pieces at a time. I'm still waiting to hear from that one courageous gallery owner willing to show my entire collection." She paused. "I plan to return to Israel next year to interview more survivors. How about you? How do you find people to interview?"

"Most are referrals from Mr. Feinberg…the most recent being Johanna. When he called, all he said was that she was a survivor of Ravensbruck. He didn't tell me she was young and pretty."

A soft grin crossed the woman's face, which to Bryan, meant that Johanna had confided in her. No matter, he liked Rita and respected her for staying true to her art.

"I have an idea," she said, after a thoughtful pause. "Can you give me the names of four or five survivors that you interviewed? Depending on what they say, I'd like to use them as subjects for my work."

Bryan smiled. "If you hadn't asked, I would have suggested it. Well, I know you want to get back to your studio." He got up to leave. "I'll call you in a couple of days."

Chapter Thirty-Four

"I finally got a chance to breathe," Helen said. "I've been working overtime and catching up on my sleep. Still interested in doing dinner?"

Bryan smiled. "Anytime," he said into the receiver.

"If you don't mind, I'd like to do it here at my place...say around seven? Nothing fancy. Just pizza and a salad."

"Sounds good to me. You make the salad, and I'll bring the pizza. See you at seven."

~ * ~

Bryan showed up with a boxed pizza and set it down on the kitchen table, next to a lit candle and an opened bottle of Chianti. He poured a little into their glasses. They ate while they talked, at first about Helen's new job and then about Bryan's recent interviews. "I also met with Johanna's friend, Rita, a Holocaust artist," he added. "She incorporates elements of a survivor's story in her art. She asked if I could provide the names of people we interviewed. I have to come up with at least five. Any ideas?" He poured some more wine into her glass and into his own.

Helen thought about it. "My first choice would be the Sonderkommando who pulled the bodies from the gas chamber and carried them to the crematorium. He did this day after day, month after month." She shook her head. "My second would be Mrs. Rosenberg, the young woman who jumped from a moving freight car. It's a miracle she wasn't badly hurt."

Bryan nodded. "The one I would choose is Ruth, the girl who survived the gas chamber at Auschwitz. I can visualize how the Sonderkommandos and the doctor fought to bring her back to life. Another would be Carl Steiner, the gay man who endured castration and humiliation at Buchenwald. People need to see they were victims, just like the Jews." He sipped his wine. "We need one more."

"What about Mr. Mendel, the Jehovah's witness. The way he described the witch of Buchenwald and her sick hobby of removing tattoos from prisoners sent shivers through my spine."

"Good choice. I'll contact Rita and give her the names."

The phone rang. She took her time getting up to answer it. "I understand." She nodded. "No problem. I'll be there as soon as I can." She hung up. "As you heard, it was the hospital. They wanted to know if I could come in a couple of hours early. One of the nurses failed to show and they haven't been able to reach her."

Unable to hide his disappointment, Bryan stood and ambled up the door.

"I think we should do it again." She grinned. "But I promise, the next time, it will be a proper dinner. I'm a pretty good cook if I do say so myself."

~ * ~

Back home, Bryan got a call from Rita. "I just spoke with Johanna. She was pleased that we got a chance to meet. When she asked if I had invited you to my upcoming birthday party, I was embarrassed to say that I hadn't. That's why I'm calling. I'd love you to attend. It'll be here at my house on Friday of next week at six o'clock."

He smiled. "Thanks, I'll put it on my calendar. Not to change the subject but I came up with five survivors who I think will make good subjects for you. Got a pen?" He gave her a couple of seconds, then read their names and phone numbers.

"I may use all of their stories…or maybe just one. What I look for is something unique, something that will make an indelible statement like the ones you saw in my house. When I'm done, you're welcome to see the results."

"Thank you. I'll look forward to it."

"Well, I won't keep you. The next time we meet will be at the party. By the way…no gifts unless they're the drinkable kind." She chuckled.

~ * ~

"Sorry to call so late," Mr. Feinberg said, "but I thought you'd want to know that we found a man who may be your grandmother's cousin, Felix Goren, from the village of Lodz."

"Where is he?" Bryan said, with restrained excitement.

"He lives in Israel under the alias Robert Kosinski. When Dachau was liberated, he seemed confused and disoriented...couldn't even remember his name. He'd suffered severe blows to the head. With the help of a Jewish organization, he and other refugees were sent to France. From there they boarded a ship bound for Palestine. Years later, he still had no memory of his life or his name before being sent to the camp."

"So, how did you find him, and how do you know it's really him...my grandmother's cousin?"

"It's a remarkable story. About a year and a half ago a Polish refugee, Hans Michnik, recognized him as they stood waiting for a bus. The two had been friends and neighbors for years. When the bus arrived, they got on and sat next to each other. For almost forty minutes, Mr. Kosinski listened as Hans tried to jog his memory. By the time they reached their destination, Mr. Kosinski had no doubt that Hans spoke the truth. Sadly, he learned that his wife and two sons died at Auschwitz. His memory gradually returned, but not entirely. He has no recollection of the day he was beaten half to death, which is probably a good thing. Anyway, I have his address and other information which you're welcome to review."

A quiet sigh. "My grandmother would've been thrilled to learn that her cousin is alive." Bryan thanked Mr. Feinberg and promised to drop by in the morning.

Chapter Thirty-Five

Mid afternoon

"Thank you," Bryan said into the receiver. "Can you arrange for the unveiling the day after tomorrow…say around ten o'clock?"

"Of course, we'll have everything ready," said the caller.

Moments later, Bryan dialed Helen. "I know it's short notice, but my grandmother's headstone just arrived. The *unveiling*, as the Jews call it, will take place at ten o'clock, the day after tomorrow. You think you can break away for an hour or two?"

"I wish I could, but I'm scheduled to work a double shift on that day. I'm sorry."

He sighed in disappointment. "Like I said, it was short notice."

"I'm glad you called. Your grandmother has been on my mind lately." She hesitated. "Before she died, she sent me a letter and requested that I not tell you about it."

"What did she say?"

"She was very sweet and gave me some advice…about what I needed to do to win you over. For whatever reason she was convinced that you and I belong together, just like she and her beloved William."

"I…don't know what to say."

"Well, I wouldn't dwell on it, though she did make me think about my life, meeting you and…" She hesitated. "I'll be off for a couple of days next week. Can we try dinner again…and I don't mean pizza." She laughed.

"Sure. Just call me the day before." He smiled as he said goodbye and hung up.

He was still smiling when the phone rang, and he picked it up in mid ring. "Hi Bryan," Johanna said. "Did Rita call you about her party?"

"We spoke yesterday. She said she had neglected to invite me the day we met at the house. Of course, I said yes."

"Good. Just wanted to make sure you'd be there. Did she mention anything else...like the exhibition of her paintings later this month in San Miguel de Allende?"

"She didn't. Is it in Mexico?"

"It's a colonial town—a mecca for artists from all over the world, about a hundred seventy miles from here. My friend Beth, who owns a gallery there, agreed to show ten paintings beginning next month. Rita will come down a couple of days before, so we can spend some time in Mexico City visiting art museums. There are dozens of them, including the Frida Kahlo Museum. You should join us. I'm sure Rita wouldn't mind."

They talked for a few minutes longer. Where before, he had looked forward to seeing Johanna again, he now questioned whether he should attend the party. Was it because of Helen and the letter she got from his grandmother? Maybe. The question nagged him the rest of the day and into the evening.

Chapter Thirty-Six

The phone rang, just after 6:00 a.m. Still in bed, Bryan reached over to answer it.

"Did you hear the news?" Bill Taylor said.

"I just got up. What happened?"

"They found O'Hara's body. It washed up on the beach south of San Diego."

It took a second for the words to sink in. "How do they know it's him?"

"He had a tattoo on his forearm that said: D-Day June 6, 1944, which police had described in a bulletin the day after he went missing. Of course, they won't know for sure until they check his dental records."

"Do you know if he had a family?"

"He was a widower with no children. I'm not sure, but I think he had a distant cousin who lived in Hawaii. He talked about moving there but changed his mind when his emphysema started to worsen."

"You knew him as well as anyone, what do you think we should do? I mean, there's no doubt that Tanya and her friends are responsible for his death."

The man sighed. "I wish I had a good answer. The reality is that Tanya and her friends are untouchable."

"That's *it*?" Bryan said, his voice rising. "I'm sorry, but I can't accept it. Surely, there's got to be a way to expose them or to at least show that O'Hara was killed because he knew too much about Nazis living in America."

"Look, I know how you feel, but there's nothing we can do. On the other hand, if you had the list, you'd have some leverage. Any chance O'Hara's friend will reach out to you again?"

Bryan shrugged. "I was kind of rough with him when he called, so, it's anybody guess what he'll do now that O'Hara's body has been identified."

"Well, whatever happens, I hope you'll let me know."

"You can count on it." Bryan placed the phone back on its hook. Seconds later, it rang again. Must've forgotten to tell me something.

"Too bad about your friend," said the caller.

Bryan recognized Joaquin's voice. "What do you want?"

"Tanya is not giving up, you know. According to my sources, O'Hara didn't tell them anything, which means that you're still being watched. Soon, maybe sooner than expected, you'll be forced to make a choice. So, I would advise that you keep my number handy." He hung up.

Chapter Thirty-Seven

Thirty-eight hours later

"Can I help you?" Bryan stood behind the partially opened door.

"My name is Jack Richards. I'm a friend of Sam O'Hara. We spoke on the phone, the day after he went missing."

Bryan hesitated. "I never thought I'd hear from you again. Come inside." They sat across from each other.

"I was here earlier. No one answered the door. To be honest, I almost didn't come back. I was afraid you wouldn't want to see me."

"I…want to apologize for the way I spoke to you before. The truth is, I didn't want to get involved any more than I already am. But things are different now. I want to hear what you have to say. As you probably know, the people who are looking for O'Hara's list are still out there. They'll not hesitate to come after either one of us. I hope you weren't followed."

"I flew in from Virginia and checked into a hotel. I took the longest way possible to get to your house. I'm sure nobody followed me." He paused. "Before O'Hara went missing, he made me promise that if anything were to happen to him, I should turn the list over to you. Like I said on the phone, he trusted you and figured you'd know what to do with it."

"So, where is it?" He sat up straight.

The man raised his hand. "One step at a time." He cleared his throat. "Can I trouble you for a glass of water?"

"Of course." Bryan got up, went to the kitchen and came back with a large glass of water. He handed it to him.

"Thanks." Richards took a couple of big gulps, then set the glass down. "To answer your question, I don't have the list with me. For my protection, I placed it inside the Bible in the drawer of the nightstand. I paid for two nights, but I'm leaving the hotel at eight in the morning. Here's the second key." He placed it on the coffee table. "You can drop by any time after eight."

Bryan picked up the key and stuck it in the dirt of a potted plant next to the couch. "You can't be too careful. There's no telling when the people who have been tailing me will show up." He paused. "How long have you known O'Hara, God rest his soul?"

Richards took another gulp of water. "We met during the war. We were part of the unit that liberated Dachau. The sight of emaciated prisoners walking around and dead bodies, including young children left lying everywhere, made most of us nauseous. Some, including O'Hara, who was as tough as they come, openly cried. Who could blame them? Nothing we'd seen before had prepared us for this." He shook his head. "Sadly, there was little we could do. We had arrived too late.

"Sam and I remained friends and stayed in contact after the war. Though we lived in separate cities, we got together at least once a year. When I got married, he was my best man and later I was his. Judy, his wife whom he met on a blind date, suffered from a heart condition. But it didn't matter to him. Over the years she got sicker and sicker until she died, not from her condition but from a viral infection she contracted during a hospital stay.

"By this time Sam had been an Immigration investigator for almost twelve years. Most of us put the war behind us as best we could, but not Sam. He complained when the government started recruiting ex-Nazis to work as spies against the Soviets. He'd seen what the Nazis had done and as far as he was concerned, they deserved to be punished, every one of them. His superiors didn't agree and after one too many battles with them, he turned in his badge. But the stress of being the *lone ranger* as he put it, took a toll on his health. He had developed a breathing disorder, which his doctor said would improve if he moved to the Southwest. Living in a hot, dry climate didn't appeal to him, so he moved to San Diego instead. Even in retirement, he fumed every time he read about ex-Nazis being captured in other countries, but not in America."

"Getting back to the list…do you know if he gave a copy to anyone else?"

Richards half-shrugged. "It's possible, I suppose. Sam had other friends besides me."

The phone rang and they stared at it for a second.

"Well, I did my duty." The man stood to leave. "What you do with the list is your business. I'll see myself out."

Bryan thanked him, then rushed to answer the phone.

"I just heard about O'Hara," Helen said. "Even though I knew he might not be alive, it came as a shock. Does this mean it's all over?"

"Not quite. Tanya and her friends are still out there." Brief pause. "There's something you should know. O'Hara's friend—the one who called the other night—just left the house. He's the last person I expected to knock at my door, especially after the way I spoke to him." Bryan filled her in on what the man had said about O'Hara and the list. "To my surprise, he didn't bring it. He was very cautious and explained that he'd left it at his hotel inside a bible in the drawer of the nightstand. Then he handed me his room key, so I could pick it up in the morning."

"Are you sure you want to do this?" she said, a tinge of concern in her voice. "Up to now you've been lucky. Maybe you should—"

"O'Hara trusted me. I'm not going to let him down. Tomorrow, I'll pick up the list and hide it where no one can find it. Then, I'll consider my options." He smiled a little. "About next week…I'm really looking forward to it."

"Me too. I'll prepare something special…from a recipe that I got from Ladies Home Journal."

The doorbell rang. "I've got to go. We'll talk later." He hung up, waited a second, then crossed the room.

"Surprised to see me?" Tanya said, a mischievous tone to her voice. "We need to talk." She walked in and followed him to the living room. She sat across from him. Her associate knew what he had to do and disappeared into the den.

"Go ahead and search…but you're wasting your time." He blinked a couple of times, averting his eyes from the potted plant.

"Cut the crap. We saw a guy leaving the house just minutes ago. You want to tell me about it?"

"He was a friend of O'Hara. I had never met him before. He…he was in town on business and decided to pay me a visit. He was concerned about the way O'Hara's death was reported. We didn't talk for long. When I said I didn't know any more than what I'd read in the paper, he got up and left. By the way, he's the one who called the cops to request a wellness check at the house."

"What's his name?"

"Jack. That's all he gave. He was very guarded, like he didn't know if he could trust me."

Tanya stared at him. "We've played this game before and it's getting old. You may think you're between the rock and the hard place, but you're not. There's only one way you'll come out of this unscathed. You know that don't you?"

Bryan's jaw muscles tightened. "You made your point. I know what I have to do."

"Good." She forced a fake smile. "Still have my number?"

"I memorized it."

Moments later, her associate emerged from one of the bedrooms. He'd searched the entire place. "Nothing. I even checked the trash and the freezer." He walked over to Bryan. "Just say the word and I'll make him talk."

"That won't be necessary." Tanya glanced around, then stood to leave.

When he heard the door shut behind them, Bryan closed his eyes and let out a sigh. He had a feeling he'd not seen the last of them.

~ * ~

Jack Richards called three hours later. "Don't go to the hotel," he said, his voice frantic. "It's not safe."

"What happened?" Bryan pressed the phone to his ear.

"After I left your house, I drove back to my hotel. When I pulled into the lot, I noticed a car with two men sitting in it, parked in the back row. I don't know why, but it made me uneasy. I waited a couple of minutes before getting out of the car. As I strode toward the entrance, I glanced over my shoulder and saw the same two men walking toward me.

Once inside, I hurried to get to my room. The first thing I did was remove the list from the Bible. Then I packed my bag and rushed out the door. I took the stairs. The men were in the lobby and so I ran out a side entrance. I had to get out of town—drove directly to Phoenix and booked the next flight back to Richmond."

"These men…the ones that followed you, do you remember anything about them?"

A brief pause. "I'm not sure, but I think one of them wore a cap like the kind they wear in Europe. It stuck with me because I bought one just like it several years ago. Come to think of it I don't know what happened to it. Anyway, that's all I remember."

Bryan frowned. *A cap like the kind they wear in Europe.* Joaquin wore a similar cap. Coincidence? He wondered. "About the list…can you mail it to me?"

"Too risky. People know where you live."

"You're right." Bryan thought about it. "I have an idea. You can send it to my friend Helen Darby. I trust her as much as I trusted O'Hara. Got a pen?" He waited a couple of seconds, then gave the address.

They agreed not to have any further contact.

Minutes later, Bryan dialed Helen's number. He told her about the list and his conversation with Jack Richards. "I suggested that he mail it to me, but he felt it would be too dangerous. That's when I thought of you." He hesitated. "I gave him your address, which I know I shouldn't have, before calling you."

"Yes, I wish you had called," she said, mildly annoyed. "No matter, what's done is done. I'll keep an eye out for it."

"Thanks for being so understanding," he said, sheepishly.

Chapter Thirty-Eight

The letter from Richards arrived four days later. Helen read through it quickly, then called Bryan. When he arrived, they sat at the kitchen table.

"It's all here." Bryan glanced through the list. "The names and aliases of twenty-seven former Nazis and their addresses." He took the paper, folded it twice, then slipped it into his back pants pocket. "In a way, I wish Tanya had found it when they searched O'Hara's condo. He'd still be alive."

"Have you thought about what you're going to do with it?"

Bryan shook his head. "I need to talk to someone…someone I can trust."

"What about Rabbi Hirsch?"

"You read my mind. Want to come along?"

"I'd like to, but I got home less than an hour ago and I need to hit the sack." She yawned, covering her mouth with her hand. "December can't come too soon. That's when I go back to a daytime schedule."

Bryan stood to leave. He thanked her and apologized again for giving out her address.

~ * ~

The secretary ushered Bryan into Rabbi Hirsch's office. From across the desk, he reached to shake the man's hand.

"Have a seat. On the phone, you were very cryptic." He furrowed his brow. "What's on your mind?"

Bryan took a moment. "It's a complicated story and after you hear it, you'll understand my dilemma." He went back to the beginning: meeting Helen for the first time, then O'Hara, Tanya and Joaquin, and more recently O'Hara's friend, Jack Richards. He became quiet as he reached into his coat pocket, pulled out the list of German names and handed it to him. "It was compiled by O'Hara who wanted me to have it. Despite being former Nazis, they were allowed to enter the country after the war."

"Have you showed this to anyone else?"

"Just my friend, Helen."

The rabbi studied the names, then gave the list back to him. "You're conflicted about what you should do, which is understandable. Well, I wish I had a simple answer for you, but I don't. Let me explain. In 1939 my uncle, Josef Hirsch, was aboard the St. Louis, a German ship carrying more than nine hundred Jewish refugees bound for Cuba. When it got there, they were turned away, and so the captain set sail for the United States. They were denied permission to land. The ship eventually returned to Europe where my uncle and other refugees were left to fend for themselves. He eventually found refuge in the Netherlands, but it was short lived. Months later, the Germans invaded the country, which left my uncle and other Jews vulnerable. Once again, they had nowhere to run." The Rabbi clasped his hands and sighed. "Soon after, Uncle Joseph was arrested and sent to Auschwitz where he died."

He adjusted his glasses. "I told this story because the Holocaust affected me, personally. My uncle used to visit us every year, from the time I was ten. An avid stamp collector, he encouraged me to start my own collection. I have fond memories of different stamps he bought for me. One in particular was an 1856 Austrian stamp that over the years has become quite valuable. But I digress, the point I'm trying to make is that since the war, many of us prayed and hoped that the monsters responsible for the deaths of six million Jews would be brought to justice. Some were, of course, but hundreds were not as evidenced by the list you showed me. We were outraged that so many were allowed to escape…to live out their lives as free men. So, when organizations like the Jews for Justice knocked on our doors asking for monetary contributions, Jews from all walks of life did not hesitate to contribute…and willingly, I might add."

"Should I infer that *you* were approached by one of these groups?"

A long silence. "Yes," the rabbi said, softly. "It was not easy for me to argue that what they planned to do was wrong on so many levels. At the time I had not yet decided to become a Rabbi. Not that it matters. What was morally wrong then is wrong today and tomorrow." He paused. "Getting back to your dilemma, I can't tell you what you should or should not do. That is for you to decide. All I ask is that you take your time. Hasty decisions are usually followed by regrets, or as my father would say, a bad decision cannot be undone."

Bryan nodded. Rabbi Hirsch made sense. For now, he'd put the list in a safe place, away from his home, and not think about it, at least for the next few days. "I want to thank you for seeing me on such short notice. I know you're busy, so I won't take any more of your time."

The rabbi smiled. "My door is always open. Just call like you did today…to make sure I'm in." Brief pause. "Before you leave, I want to show you something." He opened the bottom left drawer of the desk, removed an oversized envelope and pulled out a black notebook. "It's a diary written by my Uncle Josef. The entries were made during the entire voyage of the St. Louis. Some of the writing is blurred due to the place where it was stored—in a leaky shed that belonged to the family that hid my uncle in the Netherlands prior to his arrest. It's one of my most prized possessions, and also a sad reminder that he'd be with us today but for our government's policy to deny asylum to Jewish refugees."

"How did you get it?" Bryan said, his eyes fixed on the diary.

"About ten years ago, I was contacted by a man from the Netherlands. He said he had stumbled upon a diary written by Josef Hirsch. My uncle had wisely written my father's name and address on the inside cover. The caller had just purchased the property. Apparently, the previous owner did not know of the diary's existence. It was found underneath a pile of old books and magazines." He slid the diary toward Bryan. "Go ahead. Open it."

Bryan picked it up and glanced through the pages. "This is amazing. I'd heard about the St. Louis but knew little about its voyage." He looked up. "Have you thought about donating it to a university or museum?"

"I have." The rabbi nodded. "The truth is, I'd hate to part with it. Maybe someday I'll feel different, but for now it gives me comfort.

Sometimes I can almost feel my uncle's presence as I hold it in my hands."

Bryan closed the diary. "Given what you've told me about it, I'm reluctant to ask…may I borrow it? I'd like to read it, slowly…maybe take a note or two."

The rabbi considered it for a second. "I'll let you borrow it on one condition. That you include my Uncle Josef in the book you are writing."

Bryan smiled. "I had planned to do that anyway." He picked up the diary and put it back in the envelope. "Thank you. I'll return it within twenty-four hours."

Chapter Thirty-Nine

Bryan sat at his desk. He poured Ginger Ale into a glass, took a sip, then opened Josef Hirsch's diary.

May 14, 1939

It's two o'clock in the afternoon and we've been at sea for over 24 hours. While most of the passengers are exuberant, a few are fearful of what awaits us when we set foot in Cuba. It will be months before we know whether we can proceed to America. If our requests for asylum are not granted, we'll have no choice but to remain in Cuba—a far better alternative than returning to Germany. Already, there were rumors that Jews were being sent to labor camps never to be seen or heard from again.

May 15, 1939

All day I've been struggling with the guilt that I feel for being among the lucky few permitted to buy passage on the St. Louis. Hundreds, including entire families, were turned away. There is little hope they will find a passage on another ship. Their fate now lies in the hands of God.

May 16, 1939

I'm getting to meet and speak to other passengers, mostly in the dining hall. Each has a story to tell. We come from different backgrounds and different parts of Germany, though a great many are Berliners. At least six are veterans of the Great War. Perhaps they, more than anyone, find it difficult to accept that their patriotism no longer matters. It is a sad thing to have to leave a country where you were once thought of us as heroes.

May 17, 1939

This morning, I met a former university professor who spoke five languages, including Spanish. He and other Jewish professors had all been fired because they were Jewish. He teaches a Spanish class for beginners every morning and invited me to attend. I have no ear for languages, so I politely declined.

May 18, 1939

Earlier today, I met Rudolf Spiegel, a Jewish man and his gentile wife Fiona, originally from America. She could have stayed in Germany, safe in their home, but insisted on leaving with her husband, to face an uncertain future. They had been married less than two years and had never been apart for more than a week. Mrs. Spiegel has an older sister who lives in Chicago but won't be visiting her as she disapproved of their marriage. No matter, Mr. Spiegel and his wife are astronomers, and feel confident they will find work in America. Mrs. Spiegel prayed that their stay in Cuba will be no longer than nine months. Her husband smiled. A week before boarding the ship, they found out she was pregnant. I wished them luck.

May 19, 1939

Today, at 3:00 p.m., many of us gathered in the dining hall to listen to a retired businessman, who'd travelled to Cuba over the years, talk about his experiences. He assured us that the Cuban people are warm and hospitable, especially in the smaller towns and villages. The man talked for almost an hour, answering questions and allaying our fears that we might not be welcomed.

May 20, 1939

Kristallnacht, the night of broken glass, is still fresh in our minds. Our homes, businesses and synagogues were vandalized and countless Jews killed or arrested. We were loyal German citizens, yet we had no protection from the police or the courts. Within forty-eight hours we had to make a choice: flee or die. My friend, Oskar, was concerned, but not enough to join me when he had a chance. His grandparents live in a small town in Austria, and he went there, convinced it would be safer than Germany. I pray he is right, though I fear it is only a matter of time before the Austrians turn against their own Jewish citizens.

May 21, 1939

The children on board seem not to have a care in the world. They spend their time playing games and exploring the ship. The parents have told them as little as possible about why they left in a hurry—some in the middle of the night, with only the clothes on their backs.

May 22, 1939

Today, I got seasick and stayed in my cabin. I ventured out just before dinner, thinking the fresh air would do me good. It didn't. Not until a ship steward offered me a cup of ginger tea, did I start to feel better. Later, I had a light meal of potato soup and plain noodles.

May 23, 1939

Apparently, I was not the only passenger suffering from sea sickness. The ship's doctor has been busy treating at least twenty other passengers, including the famed scientist, Igor Cantor, who had to abandon his research in the field of genetics and immunology. Hopefully, he'll continue his work at a research facility in America. Germany's loss will be America's gain.

May 24, 1939

The captain, Gustav Schroder, is to be commended for the way he interacts with the passengers. He genuinely cares about us and goes out of his way to make sure that all our needs are being met. It is clear by his words and demeanor that he does not share his fellow countrymen's views of the Jews. Early on, he allowed us to participate in Friday prayers in the dining room and gave permission to remove the official portrait of Adolf Hitler that hung on the wall.

May 25, 1939

According to the captain, we will be in Havana within two days or less. Everyone is excited and eager to get off the ship. The first thing I'll do is mail a letter to my brother, Simon Hirsch, in America just to say I arrived. I'll explain what is happening in Germany when I see him and his family. I brought some rare stamps for my favorite nephew, Aaron, to add to his collection. He'll be pleased to know that two of them are extremely rare.

May 26, 1939

In the evening just before retiring, a knock came at the door. It was an elderly woman with an unusual request. She asked if I would accompany her once we got off the ship. She was a widow traveling alone and feared for her safety. Yes, of course, I said without hesitation. At that point she started to cry. Thank you, she said over and over again. Then she became quiet and told me her story. On the first day of Kristallnacht, an angry mob stormed into her son's jewelry shop and dragged him into the street. They beat him to death while police stood by and did nothing. The mob then returned to the shop and stole his entire inventory. Fortunately, her son kept a small bag of diamonds hidden behind her bedroom wall. The day after buying a ticket for passage on the St. Louis, she took the diamonds and sewed them into the lining of her coat. She'll wear the same coat on the day we disembark in Havana. She didn't have to tell me about it, but I'm glad she did.

The phone rang and he picked it up in mid-ring. "Good news," Helen said. "There's been a change in my schedule. Can you come for dinner the day after tomorrow?"

"Sure. What time?"

"Seven-thirty. Hate to run, but I'm late for a dental appointment."

Bryan smiled. He hung up and resumed reading.

May 27, 1939

When the ship finally arrived in Havana there appeared to be a problem on the docks. According to the captain, Cuban authorities had invalidated the ship's landing permits. We were ordered to stay on the ship.

May 28, 1939

In the morning, the captain learned that the fate of the passengers' rests in the hands of certain high level officials who fear we'll become a burden to Cuba's struggling economy. Again, we were told to remain on the ship. For how long, no one could say.

May 29, 1939

It's been three days. We've heard nothing from Cuban officials. According to the captain, a number of Jewish Cubans living in Havana are prepared to sponsor some of the refugees. As they have no influence on anyone in power, their offer will likely be rejected. Still, there is hope that at least families with children may be allowed to disembark.

May 30, 1939

Still, no word from anyone. The captain is at a loss to explain why we are not allowed to disembark, if only temporarily. When pressed by some of the passengers, he admitted that some government officials are reluctant to accept Jewish refugees for fear that others will follow.

May 31, 1939

Sometime in the middle of the night, a young man jumped into the ocean. He tried to swim ashore but was quickly apprehended by Cuban authorities that patrol the waters. They brought him back, soaking wet, and turned him over to the captain. The incident is likely to discourage others from trying to leave the ship by any means.

June 1, 1939

No one, not even the captain, knows what tomorrow will bring. So, we sit and wait. God help us if the Cubans decide to turn us away.

June 2, 1939

This morning, the captain announced that the Cuban government had decided not to grant our requests for asylum. The decision was final. Captain Schroder had no choice but to cast off and look for another port. One passenger was so distraught that he tried to kill himself. He was taken to the nearest hospital and remained there as the St. Louis set sail for the United States 90 miles away. When we came within view of the Florida Coast, the U.S. Coast Guard appeared and ordered the captain to turn the ship around. The United States would not accept the refugees under any circumstance. Disappointed, the captain then set sail for Canada.

The ship was two days from Halifax harbor when the captain received an urgent message: the Canadian government would not allow the passengers to disembark. Reluctantly, and under pressure from his superiors in Germany, the captain set a course for Hamburg.

June 3, 1939

All hope was lost when America and Canada turned their backs on us. We are now officially stateless. If the passengers were gentiles, would the outcome be any different? It is a question that begs for an answer that no one is ready to accept.

June 4, 1939

I couldn't sleep and woke up earlier than usual. My thoughts ran from anger to bitterness and frustration. I am fearful of what awaits us when we return to Germany.

In the afternoon, I walked the upper deck and met a middle-aged man, traveling alone. He'd heard a rumor the day before that the ship had changed its course to a neutral port in Lisbon. Throughout the day, I heard similar rumors from other passengers. Later, as we took our seats in the dining room, the captain stood up and made an announcement. He'd heard the rumors and wished to put them to rest. "We are on course for Hamburg, with no scheduled stops in Lisbon or any other port," he said. The room became suddenly quiet. After a moment, at least half of the passengers got up and walked out.

June 5, 1939

Before breakfast, the captain suggested that we form a committee that would speak for the passengers. They will be free to speak to him about a variety of issues and concerns that are likely to arise in the days to come. I was invited to be on the committee. Already, I had considered talking to him concerning, yet another rumor that has been circulating since we left Cuba: that Jewish leaders from the United States have been trying to find countries willing to take some or all of the refugees. I will bring this up when we have our first meeting with him tomorrow afternoon.

June 6, 1939

The committee, made up of three men and two women, met with the captain at exactly 3:30 p.m. as he requested. We sat at a table in the empty dining room. From the very beginning, the captain made us feel at ease and encouraged us to speak freely about any topic. After a pause, a man raised his hand. Someone had scrawled the words DIRTY JEW on his bathroom mirror while he and his wife were away. Another said the same thing happened to him, and to at least two other passengers.

"I'm glad you brought this to my attention," the captain said. He promised to look into it and assured us that this would not happen again. After a moment, I raised my hand and said that since leaving Cuba, word had begun to spread about Jewish-American organizations trying to find countries willing to take us. Is this true? I asked. The captain chose his words carefully. He'd heard that people behind the scenes were in contact with various European countries. That's all he knew. He apologized for his inability to provide further details. Though he didn't say much, it gave me hope that a miracle might yet happen.

June 7, 1939

During breakfast, I sat next to an elderly widower. His wife of 50 years had died the year before. He admitted that he would rather kill himself than return to Germany. "Better to die on your own terms than at the hands of the Nazis," he blurted. Afterwards, I couldn't get the man's words out of my mind. Was it a sentiment shared by other passengers? I wondered. And I wondered if I would have similar thoughts the closer we got to Germany.

Later, I spoke with a young couple who had been married less than a month. You could tell they were in love. When I asked if they were worried about their future, the woman smiled and said, "It's in God's hands. What will be, will be." She's right, of course. It's out of our hands. All we can do is pray.

A pall of uncertainty hangs over us. Yet, life on the ship goes on as usual. Except for the children, everyone wears a face that belies the fear that they feel. For some, deep prayer and counseling by a rabbi on board, helps them get through the day. I envy them. Their faith keeps them from dwelling on things over which they have no control.

June 8, 1939

Returning to my cabin after a morning walk, I spotted a note someone had slipped under the door. I picked it up. Written by the widow who had sought my help earlier in the voyage, it said, "I need to see you. Please come to my cabin." When I got there, she went straight to the point. She feared that if arrested in Hamburg, the authorities would find and confiscate her diamonds. Once again, she asked for my help. What if we put them in a box and mail it to my brother in America, I said. I'll give it to the captain with instructions that he mail it after we disembark in Hamburg. My brother will keep the diamonds until you let him know where to send them.

"The captain may betray us or keep the diamonds," she said.

He's proved to be a good, honorable man, I replied. I would trust him with my life. Reluctantly, the woman agreed to the plan.

Bryan paused to reflect on a term he'd heard many times, since the end of the war: *The Good German*, a generic phrase meant to describe the hundreds, if not thousands of ordinary Germans who opposed Hitler, either secretly or overtly. The term aptly applied to Captain Schroder.

June 9, 1939

144

Earlier in the day, I stood on the upper deck, peering out into the distance. "Can you help me?" said a small voice from behind. I turned around. A young girl holding a bottle in her hand asked if I would throw the bottle into the ocean for her. It contained a written message. I obliged and threw it out as far as I could. She walked away before I could ask what she had written.

Later, I was approached by a young man who'd overheard an older couple discussing plans to jump into the ocean. Maybe it's just talk, I said. The man shrugged, then added that he'd heard similar conversation throughout the ship. Though it was disturbing to hear, I didn't want to bring it to the attention of the captain, just yet. Maybe I'll speak to the rabbi and ask his opinion.

June 10, 1939

Today, the committee met to discuss a troubling report about a group of passengers who planned to take over the bridge and force the captain to set sail for England. The details were sketchy. As improbable as it appeared, we agreed that the captain should be notified.

Later, when the captain joined us, we told him what little we knew about the mutinous plot. He did not act surprised. "Desperate people do desperate things," he said. He urged us to stay vigilant and report anything that might endanger the crew or the passengers.

Afterwards, we spoke to one of the plotters, a 23-year-old man whose identity was withheld from the captain. When we explained that we had exposed their ill-conceived plot, he almost seemed relieved. He assured us that for the rest of the voyage, there would be no more talk about taking over the bridge.

June 11, 1939

During lunch we had the pleasure of listening to a trio of violinists who had played for the Berlin Philharmonic. They were fired shortly after Kristallnacht. We learned later that the captain had personally requested that they play for the passengers. We also learned that one of them had vowed to throw his Stradivarius violin overboard, minutes before arriving in Germany. Who could blame him? Better in the ocean than in the hands of the Nazis.

June 12, 1939

The committee meets daily to discuss problems and issues that are brought before us. Today we heard from a man who claimed that his 17-year-old daughter had been violated by a crewmember. Did she tell you this? I asked. "Not in so many words," he replied. "A father knows about these things. She's afraid and bursts into tears when I press her for answers."

The committee was in agreement. Without proof or the girl coming forward, we could not go to the captain and expect him to investigate the alleged violation. With your permission, I said, we would like to speak to your daughter. "I won't allow it," he said, adamantly. "I insist that you notify the captain at once." We stood firm and told him that unless we spoke to his daughter, there was nothing we could do. The man relented. Moments later, he showed up with the girl. We asked to speak to her alone. He objected. Again, we stood firm, and he left in a huff. It didn't take long for the truth to come out. She'd been having a secret affair with a boy she knew from school. Her father would not have approved, and so she let him believe it was a crewmember. We had no choice but to tell the father, and the matter was put to rest.

June 13, 1939

Most of the passengers remain stoic. Some stay in their cabins, sometimes for hours. While others enjoy walking the decks or sitting in lounge chairs. Few children play as before. They know intuitively that all is not right. They ask questions but get nebulous answers. God help them and the rest of us as we try to get from one day to the next, hoping and praying for some kind of miracle.

June 14, 1939

Early this morning the captain made an important announcement. He'd just learned that England, the Netherlands, Belgium and France had offered to accept Jewish refugees. Stunned, we could hardly believe it. God had answered our prayers. We cried and held each other until the captain made another announcement. Against orders from his superiors, he would bypass Hamburg and set sail for the port of Antwerp, Belgium. It is true. God works in mysterious ways.

June 15, 1939

People are smiling again. We'll soon be in Belgium. Some will stay in the country, while others will make their way to England, the Netherlands and France. I have friends in the Netherlands, so that's where I will go. But I'll not stay long. I MUST find a way to get to America.

June 16, 1939

Late last night a passenger died from an undisclosed ailment. He had been ill since boarding the ship. His hope for recovery in a Cuban hospital faded when authorities turned the St. Louis away. Pending funeral arrangements, his widow will remain in Antwerp, indefinitely.

June 17, 1939

We have arrived! The nightmare is over. Can't wait to get off the ship. I don't know if I will continue writing the journal as I may be too busy trying to build a new life for myself in the Netherlands.

Bryan sat there for a moment, then closed the diary and slipped it into the envelope. Later, in a call to Rabbi Hirsch, he proposed an alternative to donating it to a university or Holocaust Museum, something the rabbi had been reluctant to do. "Why not lend it to them—as a tribute to your uncle—for a specific period of time? Private art collectors and dealers do this all the time. The diary will always be yours to keep."

"As a tribute to my uncle…hmm…I like the sound of it. When you come in tomorrow, let's talk about it."

Bryan smiled as he hung up and leaned back in his chair.

Chapter Forty

Two days later

"If you're still hungry, there's another chop on the stove," Helen said.

"Thanks, but two is my limit, especially after the hefty portion of mashed potatoes that you put on my plate." Bryan patted his stomach.

"I can wrap it up, if you'd like."

"Sure, I'll have it for lunch tomorrow." He grinned. "You were right. You *are* a good cook."

She smiled. "Let's go into the living room. But give me a minute while I put everything away."

Bryan sipped the last of his wine, then stepped across to the couch.

"So, how did it go…your meeting with Rabbi Hirsch?" Helen sat beside him.

"His reaction was not what I expected. Turns out that he had an uncle who was a passenger on the St. Louis—the ship that was turned away when it reached American waters in 1939. Some called it the voyage to nowhere." He paused. "Rabbi Hirsch made it clear that the Holocaust had affected him personally and profoundly, as he was very close to his uncle. He then showed me a diary that his Uncle Josef had written throughout the entire voyage."

"Did you read it?"

"Rabbi Hirsch allowed me to borrow it. I returned it the following day. I'm embarrassed to say that I knew very little about the St. Louis and its passengers." He sighed. "It was difficult to read, knowing that so many ended up in the gas chambers of Auschwitz. Maybe I'll ask if he'd consider making a copy, so that others can read it."

"What did he say about O'Hara's list?"

"He understood my dilemma but didn't give any advice, except that I should let my conscience be my guide. I'm glad I talked to him, though. I learned that he knew about the JFJ—even admitted he had been approached by them years ago before becoming a rabbi."

She looked at him. "Just so I'm clear…you're not seriously thinking about giving the list to Joaquin, are you?"

He hesitated. "I won't lie to you. I've not ruled it out."

"I think you're letting your obsession with the Nazis cloud your thinking. Maybe you should table it…indefinitely. Better yet, destroy the list while you still can."

"I wish it were that easy. Too much has happened since you showed me Muller's deathbed confession. But don't worry, I'm in no hurry to hand it over to Joaquin or anyone else, for that matter."

"I'm glad you said that, though I'd feel better if you had an alternative plan."

"I'm working on one." He nodded. "That's all I can say for now. I promise that whatever I decide to do, you'll be the first to know."

"Good." She smiled. "Now let me tell you the latest. This morning my supervisor informed me that I would be working the day shift beginning next week, which came as a total surprise. Isn't that great? I'll have my nights free to do what I want."

"This calls for a celebration. You pick the day and I'll take you to dinner."

"I know just the place; a French restaurant called Le Petit Paris that I've always wanted to try."

"Great. It's a date."

For the rest of the evening, the conversation remained light, almost playful. When it was time for him to leave, he leaned closer as though to kiss her but held back. Too soon, he thought, considering they were *just friends*.

~ * ~

In the morning, Bryan got a call from Rita, reminding him of her birthday party, less than a week away. "I just talked to Johanna, and she's looking forward to seeing you again."

He'd already decided to skip it but thanked her for letting him know. Later, he regretted that he didn't give an excuse, any excuse, for not being able to attend.

Chapter Forty-One

Joaquin sat at a table toward the back of the Chinese restaurant, waiting for Nicolas to appear. He sipped black tea and checked his watch. The man was late. He'd give him five more minutes and then...he spotted him as he came through the door. Tall and muscular, with a military bearing, Nicolas nodded and made his way to the table. "I thought I had a tail and went a mile out of my way to get here. You can't be too careful."

"Never mind about that," Joaquin said, an impatient tone to his voice. "Bring me up to date."

"All the men are in place, scattered across the country, waiting for orders. Half came from Europe. Most lost entire families."

"We've talked about it before, but if anything should go wrong—"

"Not to worry. They know the risks. If arrested they'll say nothing."

Joaquin reached into his pants pocket and pulled out a piece of paper with an address scribbled across it. He handed it to him. "It's a safe house in West Texas…just in case they need a place to cool off."

The man took the paper and slipped it in his wallet. "You should know," he hesitated, "that some of the men are getting restless. I don't know what to tell them."

A brief silence. "Tell them that if I don't have the list of Nazis by the end of the week, they're under no obligation to stay. I'll not hold it against those who wish to return to their jobs and families."

"I'll repeat what you said, but I can assure you that every man is committed to staying with us for as long as necessary. All they want is to hear that the mission is still viable."

"It most definitely is." He slapped his hand on the table. "They mustn't get discouraged. Tell them …tell them that I expect to receive the list of names at any moment." Not entirely the truth, but under the circumstances, he had to at least appear that he had everything under control.

The man nodded. "Now let's talk about some of the problems we're likely to encounter."

~ * ~

Later, in a call to Mr. Feinberg, Joaquin admitted being under pressure to produce O'Hara's list. "I know you don't want to be personally involved, but we need your help. All you have to do is talk to Bryan, preferably at his house. Find out if he has O'Hara's list. Can you do that?"

"I'll drop by this evening." He paused. "But don't be surprised if I leave empty-handed."

"Just do your best." He hung up.

Chapter Forty-Two

When Bryan opened the door just after 8:00 p.m., the last person he expected to see was Mr. Feinberg. "I know it's late, but I have to speak to you. May I come in?"

"Of course. By the look on your face, it must be important." They sat in the living room.

"I had planned to make up a story about the reason for my visit, but…" He took a deep breath. "I won't lie to you. I'm here because I know about O'Hara's list."

"Let me guess." Bryan frowned. "Joaquin sent you to find out if I had it."

An exasperated sigh. "We're all on the same side, are we not? Before you answer, let me tell you my story. You've heard everyone else's, so why not mine? I promise I'll be brief."

Bryan crossed his arms. "I'm listening."

"The day it happened…when a young German officer and two soldiers burst into my home, I froze, literally. I could not move a muscle. Not even when one of the soldiers walked into the bedroom and found my eldest daughter taking a nap. 'Wake up', he yelled. The next thing I hear is screaming—my daughter crying and calling out to me. The soldier laughed as he beat her into submission, raping her and then inviting the other soldier to do the same. All the time, I did nothing. I carry the guilt that I should have done something, even if it meant sacrificing my life." He bowed his head. "It's a memory that haunts me to this day, even in my dreams."

"I'm sorry," Bryan said, softly.

Mr. Feinberg clenched his jaw "You were right. Joaquin asked me to talk to you. I'm a bitter man because of what happened to me and my family, and the only thing that keeps me going is the hope that someday soon, a few ex-Nazis will get what they justly deserve."

"I've not walked in your shoes, so I'm not in a position to judge." He drew a slow breath. "You took a gamble coming here, hoping I would help you. I appreciate your honesty, but even if I had O'Hara's list, I'm not sure I would give it you. The truth is, I need more time to consider all options."

"I know O'Hara was your friend. I also know he was passionate about exposing Nazi criminals across the country." He hesitated. "What would he do?"

Bryan thought about it. "He would probably give you the names. But I'm not him, and I don't want to be forced into making a decision that I might regret for the rest of my life."

Mr. Feinberg rose to his feet. "I guess there's nothing more to say. If you change your mind, you have my number."

Bryan remained seated. For a second, he wished they had talked a little longer. But under the circumstances, it was just as well they didn't. He might've weakened and turned the list over to him.

~ * ~

From across the street, Tanya and her associate watched as Mr. Feinberg got into his car and drove away. "This may be our lucky night," she said. "Follow him. He was here for a reason and if I'm right..." She half-smiled. "Let's pull him over."

They were behind less than a car's length when Mr. Feinberg suddenly accelerated.

"Go alongside him," she said. The two cars were side by side, now. She thrust a gun in his direction. "Pull over, pull over," she shouted. The frightened man drove even faster. Failing to slow for a curve just ahead, he lost control and slammed into a tree.

Tanya and her associate quickly got out of their own car and rushed to the crumpled vehicle. Mr. Feinberg's bloody, lifeless body lay half in and half out on the driver's side. "Find the list," she ordered.

Her associate searched through the man's shirt and pants pocket.

"Nothing. All he had was his wallet and a pack of cigarettes."

She frowned. "If he didn't have it, then why did he try to get away from us?"

"Beats me." The man shrugged. "Maybe he thought we wanted to rob him."

She glanced around. "Let's get out of here." They got back in the car and sped away.

Chapter Forty-Three

In the morning, Bryan turned on the TV and caught the end of a news report from the field. "There were no witnesses, and it is believed that speed was a factor in the crash that killed sixty-two-year-old Oskar Feinberg," said the reporter. The phone rang and he picked it up on the first ring.

"Did you hear about Mr. Feinberg?" Helen said.

"I just saw it on the news. He dropped by my house last night. We talked for a few minutes, and then he left. The road he took home was dark. He would not have been speeding. It makes no sense."

"Unless he feared for his life."

"I think you're right. He admitted that Joaquin had asked him to pay me a visit, hoping I would give him the list. Of course, I told him I didn't have it. Tanya and her goon must have followed him." He gave a heavy sigh. "Poor man. He survived the Holocaust only to die, frightened and alone on a darkened road."

"So, what are you going to do?"

"Well, I can't go to the police. I'd have to tell them all about Tanya and O'Hara's list. It would go over their heads."

"I see what you mean."

A brief silence. "I never told you, but before Mr. Feinberg came to see me, I had considered giving him the list for safekeeping. In a way, I wish I had. It would have been out of my hands and off my conscience."

~ * ~

Joaquin's call didn't come as a surprise. "Are you going to let them get away with it?" His tone was calm, almost friendly. "I don't know if you gave Mr. Feinberg the list, but if you didn't, now is the time to do what's right. You owe it to him, and to all the survivors that you interviewed." Brief pause. "We can't forgive, and we will *never, never forget*. Don't let us down." A short silence and then a click as Joaquin hung up the phone.

For the rest of the morning, Bryan couldn't get Joaquin's call out of his mind. On impulse, he grabbed his keys and left the house. He needed to clear his head. In the past, a drive through the desert made him see things more clearly. As he turned onto Spanish Trail, heading east toward the Rincon Mountains, his thoughts seemed to jump from one thing to another. Not until he reached an old, abandoned cemetery, did he realize that by helping Joaquin and the JFJ there would be neither winners nor losers.

Driving back to town, he still didn't know what to do. He was less than a mile from home when he turned onto the road where Mr. Feinberg had crashed his car into a tree. Someone had left a bouquet of flowers near a makeshift memorial. He pulled off to the side and sat there for a moment. The man had died for no good reason. That was all he could think of, even hours later as he watched the full report about the accident. When it was over, his mind reeled back to the beginning when he first met Oskar Feinberg. Perhaps, Joaquin was right. He owed it to him, so that his death will not have been in vain. After a moment, he poured himself a shot of brandy, downed it, and poured himself another. Then he picked up the phone and dialed Joaquin.

Chapter Forty-Four

Thirty-six hours later
Chicago

A man dressed in a dark-colored suit, strode up to a duplex with a FOR SALE sign on the lawn. He rang the bell. Seconds later, a woman wearing a long, pink robe came to the door.

"Sorry to bother you. I'm looking to buy a house in the area." He flashed a quick smile. "May I speak to Mr. Brandt?"

"Have you talked to the realtor?"

"I'd rather not. I'm prepared to make an all-cash offer if we can come to an agreement. "

She hesitated. "Wait just a moment. I'll let you speak to my husband."

A balding, heavy-set man in his mid to late fifties soon appeared. "My wife said you were interested in making a cash offer." He paused. "What did you have in mind?"

The gunman pulled out a pistol and fired two rounds into Wilhelm Brandt's head, then turned and walked briskly toward a waiting car.

~ * ~

Brooklyn

A tall, slender man in a gray uniform got off the elevator and walked to apartment 212, at the end of the hall. He rang the bell. When the door opened, he forced a friendly smile. "I have a special delivery for Mr. Hans Clauberg." He carried an oversized envelope and a small clipboard with a pen attached to it.

"I am Hans Clauberg," he said, nodding.

"Please, sign here." The man handed him the clipboard, then reached for his pistol. He pointed it at Clauberg and pulled the trigger. The gun jammed. A struggled ensued and they struggled back and forth until the man balled his fist and struck Clauberg in the jaw, causing him to fall backwards. Shaken and out of breath, the gunman ran down the stairs and out of the building.

~ * ~

Miami Beach

A short, pudgy man wearing gray pants and a blue blazer walked up the stairs of the two-story building. Otto Kramer lived in unit 202, facing the ocean. After pressing the bell, he waited a second, then pressed it again.

"Who is it?" a woman's voice said, from the behind the closed door. She spoke with a thick German accent.

"My name is Karl Becker, a fellow German. I need to speak to Mr. Kramer to warn him about a possible threat to his life. If you'll open the door, I'll explain everything."

Slowly, the door opened a bit. "Are you with the government?" she asked, a cautious tone to her voice.

"I belong to the Aryan Knights of the Fatherland…I'm sure you've heard of them."

"My husband left about thirty minutes ago to pick up a prescription. If you want, you can give me your phone number, and I'll have him call you."

The man smiled. "That won't be necessary. I'll come back later." He turned and walked back the way he had come.

"Kramer wasn't home…left to run an errand, half an hour ago," the gunman said, getting into the passenger's side of a silver VW parked directly across the street. "All we can do is wait."

The driver nodded, but didn't say anything.

Ten minutes later, a black Mercedes rolled down the street, slowed and pulled into a slot in front of the building. "It could be our guy," said the gunman. He watched as a tall, blond-haired man carrying something in his hand, made his way toward the stairs. "Start the engine." He stepped out of the car, crossed the street, and strode toward him. "Mr. Kramer," he called. The man turned around. "Who are you? What do you want?"

The gunman stepped closer, drew his gun and fired two shots, one to the head, the other to the chest. He glanced around, then hurried back to the car.

~ * ~

New Orleans

The ornate sign above the entrance read: Oasis Care & Wellness Center. Located less than a mile from the French Quarter, the two-story building looked more like a vintage hotel than a nursing home.

"I'm here to visit a friend," the gunman man said, from across the receptionist's desk. "His name is Wilhelm Lutze."

The receptionist checked her computer. "I'm sorry, but Mr. Lutze passed away late last night."

"Are you sure?" he said, a hint of disappointment in his voice.

She nodded. "The entry indicates that Mr. Lutze suffered a massive heart attack, from which he did not recover. He was pronounced dead at ten-forty-six."

The man backed away, then turned and hurried out of the building.

~ * ~

Cincinnati

The gunman smiled. "*Guten morgen.*" He ambled up to an unsuspecting middle-aged man trimming a hedge. "I'm looking for Werner Reinhardt. A friend from Germany told me that he lives at this address."

A look of suspicion filled the man's face. "Your friend is mistaken.

160

He doesn't live here."

The gunman stepped closer "What about Werner Strauss? That's what he calls himself these days."

An uncomfortable pause. "You should leave, or I'll call the police."

"Go ahead. Call the cops, and I'll tell them that you're a former Nazi responsible for killing innocent men, women and children." He pulled out a pistol and pointed it at him.

The man's face turned pale. "Please, I'm begging you. I have a wife and children."

"I had a wife and children, once. They were killed at Auschwitz." His hand started to shake, and he stepped back, as though unable to pull the trigger.

"Shoot him!" shouted the driver of a car parked nearby. Seconds passed and the gunman, still did not fire. Finally, the driver got out, walked up to the gunman, grabbed his pistol and shot Strauss twice in the head.

"I froze...I'm sorry," the gunman said, back in the car. "I thought it would be easy, but it wasn't."

"Forget it," the driver said as he shifted into gear and drove away.

By the end of the day, all but two of the shooters had killed their targets.

Chapter Forty-Five

Two days later

As was her custom after getting home from work, Helen sat at the kitchen table, sipped on a cup of chamomile tea and skimmed through the morning paper. An article on the second page caught her attention:

MURDER OF GERMAN IMMIGRANTS' SPARKS OUTRAGE

Authorities across the country are baffled by the cold-blooded murder of German Immigrants in cities across the country. In each case, a man rang the victim's doorbell, confirmed his identity, then pulled out a pistol and shot him dead. The motive for the killings remains unclear. However, according to a credible source who wished to remain anonymous, the victims all had something in common. They were former Nazis who were allowed to enter the United States, shortly after the war. The same source speculated that the killers may have been members of an underground anti-Nazi organization called Jews for Justice, or JFJ. So far, law enforcement officials have refused to comment on the anonymous source's assessment of the senseless murders.

Helen re-read the article, then dialed Bryan. "Did you give the names to Joaquin?" she said, an accusatory tone to her voice. "It came out in the paper."

A muted sigh. "It's better if we talk in person. Why don't you come over?" He hung up.

~ * ~

A half hour later, Bryan answered a call. "Listen to me. You're in danger," Joaquin said, almost shouting. "You must leave the house. Get out of there, now!"

The doorbell rang. "Hold on. It's probably Helen." He put the phone down.

"You had to do it, didn't you?" Tanya said with a pistol in her hand. Her tone matched her somber expression. She stepped inside. "I was beginning to like you. But, as they say in our business, it's not personal. You understand that don't you?"

Bryan felt the blood drain from his face. "Please...let me explain..."

"It's too late. You had your chance, and you blew it."

She pointed the pistol at his head and pulled the trigger. Bryan slumped to the floor. The receiver lay on the breakfast counter, and she walked over and picked it up, pressed it to her ear. "What's happening?" Joaquin said, still on the line. "Hello? Hello? Are you all right?"

Chapter Forty-Six

"It's been two weeks and I'm still in a daze," Helen said, from across the table in Sylvia's kitchen. "I can't eat; I can't sleep. Even at work I get distracted." She shook her head. "I thought about taking some time off, maybe go to Mexico or some other place."

"I think the grief will stay with you, no matter where you go. You can't run away from it, Helen. It's something you have to get through, one day at a time." She sighed. "Sometimes I wish I had never introduced you to Bryan. He'd be alive today."

"You're being too hard on yourself. Who could've predicated that his research would put him in the middle of a no-win situation that would cost him his life? He chose to help Joaquin and the JFJ, and I have to respect him for that. Had I not met Bryan, I would have remained blissfully ignorant of the pain and suffering those millions of men, women and children had to endure." She became quiet for a moment. "It's difficult for me to admit this, but despite what I've said in the past…Bryan and I were more than just friends. I think he felt the same way." She paused, then added, wistfully, "We'll never know what might have been."

A long silence. "What will happen to Bryan's project?"

Helen shrugged. "I don't know of anyone who would want to take it over."

"Would that include you?" Sylvia's lips formed a quiet smile. "You were there from the beginning. You were his partner, friend and confidant. I mean, who else would have the passion to continue what he started? It would be a shame to let his research go to waste."

Helen considered it for a moment. "You have a point. But I'm not a writer, and it would take a lot of work." She shook her head. "I don't know. I'll have to think about it."

~ * ~

Three days later

Tanya got up around 6:00 a.m., slipped into her sweats and hurried out the door. As she did every morning, she ran through the neighborhood of her gated community, down one street and up another, then circled back to her condo—exactly thirty-five minutes later. Still breathing hard, she unlocked the door and froze.

"It's been a long time," Joaquin said, pointing a pistol at her.

"You…you don't have to do this," she stammered. "They'll come after you."

"I'll take my chances." The gun fired and she dropped to the floor. He stood over her for a second, muttered something under his breath, and then calmly walked out of the house.

Epilogue

A month and a half later, Helen took over Bryan's project. After reviewing all of his notes and summaries of survivors' stories, she published a book about their experiences. Titled, *No More Tears To Shed*, she dedicated it to the memory of Bryan De Luca, Sam O'Hara and Oskar Feinberg. The book's starkly dark cover, designed by Holocaust artist Rita Bianco, showed a terrified Jewish prisoner trying to scale an electrified fence at Buchenwald.

In a second edition, published on the 25th anniversary of the liberation of Auschwitz, Helen included photographs of thirty victims, mostly children—some as young as three years. Their names are unknown as are the names of thousands of Jews killed in the Holocaust. Unless survivors who knew them come forward, Helen pleaded, their identities will forever be lost. A new cover, designed by Rita Bianco, depicted a ghostly image of a Jewish prisoner, floating above the entrance to Auschwitz and its iconic sign: *Arbeit Macht Frei,* Work Will Make You Free.

Following Tanya's death, Joaquin went into hiding. Left without a leader, the JFJ eventually disbanded. It resurfaced in the mid-1970s under the direction of an Auschwitz survivor from Israel. As of 1978, the JFJ was still active, mostly in South America, where they claimed credit for the assassinations of three former Nazis and the wounding of another. Though unconfirmed, the other man was believed to be the elusive Angel of Death, Dr. Josef Mengele.

About the Author

Ernesto Patino grew up in El Paso, Texas. He is a multi-genre author whose books range from Mysteries and Thrillers to Romance and Children's books. He lives in Southern Arizona with his wife Pamela, with whom he shares a passion for ethnic cuisines, classical music and foreign films. For more information about Ernesto, please visit his website at www.ernestopatino.com.

www.ingramcontent.com/pod-product-compliance
Lightning Source LLC
Chambersburg PA
CBHW070325130626
46556CB00007B/2742